DANCING WITH THE
SANDMAN

DANCING WITH THE SANDMAN

L. T. Garvin

Crystal Publishing LLC
Fort Collins, Colorado

Dancing with the Sandman

2018 ©COPYRIGHT Lana Broussard
2018 ©COVER COPYRIGHT Crystal Publishing LLC
Edited by Keri De Deo, Bonnie Walker, Claire Shepherd
Cover design by lotusdesign.biz

Published by Crystal Publishing LLC
Fort Collins, Colorado
ISBN 978-1-942624-25-7
Library of Congress Control Number: 2017950941

Dedicated with much love and gratitude to:
Twillia and Lola

By the Same Author

Confessions of a 4th Grade Athlete
Animals Galore
"A Night at Bailey's Grocery" *Texas Writers Journal*

"Time . . . thou ceaseless lackey to eternity."

William Shakespeare

Contents

1 Progress

SPLAT! Hit one ghost. Then another one. I really hate it when they grab hold and refuse to let go. Tenacious little things, aren't they? Flitting specks of blurring memories ... people, places, past lives with a pulse of resistance. So here I am driving down the new, dramatically improved, and thoroughly modern interstate highway, formerly a small two-lane road known as 82 West, where I find myself dodging ghosts.

You know exactly what I mean—those mischievous specters that flit in and out of our consciousness and play "what if" games with our memories. They must have seen me coming, and they weren't going to give up. I didn't choose to chase these flittering poltergeists.

Some I definitely would like to set free, but I find myself inevitably drawn toward these ghosts of memories past.

Slowly approaching the curve going into Kahler County, Texas, I see the old, abandoned highway 82 West off to my right. It has been isolated sufficiently from the new interstate highway. To make it there, you would have to board a time capsule to get back to what it once was and to the world where former lives intertwined, one with another. Nevertheless, a driver can exit the ultra-modern roadway and cruise right into the small Texas town that simultaneously harbors my memories and haunts my past.

Living in West Texas was never easy, or, for that matter, comfortable. This realization comes to me when I get out of the car and walk down the newly revamped sidewalks that now line the downtown. These new pavements are courtesy of the federal government: compensation for the superhighway coming in and basically killing off the town. Oh, sure, they took photos of the townsmen and immortalized their images in the concrete overpass that borders this little town. I suppose that isn't really a bad price to pay for the highway. It's just a pity that there won't be anyone left to enjoy these fabulous walkways.

When I was a small girl, that guy on the radio sang about falling into a RING OF FIRE. You know, that place where the flames of fire enfold and erase all? I actually thought he was speaking directly to us in Viney, Texas, a small, dusty town inside a county that seemed to be whatever there was of the world. I had no knowledge of anything beyond the county line.

Oh, it's not a bad little place. If you like peace and quiet, it might suit you just fine. My main regret was that the founding pioneers did not have the foresight to plant trees or much other greenery of any kind. Maybe they simply did not know there were such things as drought tolerant plants, but even if they had planted cacti, that would have been at least *something*. I won't even begin with the wind and the dust. Like the drab sparseness, they are products of the land. The Germans, the English, and the Scots-Irish settlers thought they were pulling off a coup when they wrestled this land from the Indians. In reality, the Indians were probably laughing all along: those white-skinned intruders with their funny sounding speech definitely deserved this part of the Texas prairie.

The rural environment itself doesn't bother me much, and it didn't bother me at all when I was growing up. It was a haven of sorts; the rural farm living did much to establish the principles and the substance of the all-important American work ethic. Sometimes the stillness there does a good job of filling my soul by listening to the sound of whippoorwills and looking around in all directions for miles and miles beyond. Then there is the sunset; don't even get me started on a West Texas sunset.

It is in such places where you find stories, those interwoven into the core of existence. Every place and every time has a story to tell. As for Kahler County, the people here had wholesome lives. They lived and lost in this part of the country, bounded by the romance of the early cowboys and cemented in the blood and muddy hands of the early settlers who braved Indians, uncertainty, and the cruel climate that brought many of us here in the first place.

2 Encountering Big Daddy, Once Again

Wouldn't you know, here I was at the end of the universe pondering this certain sparseness of time and place when of course I ran into someone I never expected. He was the last person on the planet I would ever dream of seeing again, but there he was walking down the sidewalk on a day hot enough to melt tree sap. I was helping my mother move out of her apartment, and to be sure, the way it goes in a small town, curiosity always draws out people. As he approached, I noticed how he had aged, and my own hand subconsciously found its way to my face. His hair was still long but graying now and pulled back into a ponytail. His skin was the same mellow brown it was back then except a bit more mottled now. Basically, he was just like I remembered: all rock'n'roll and still rather wild in faded jeans and a wrinkled plaid shirt. He smiled at me briefly through age and a missing tooth.

"This is your mother, right?" he pointed toward the apartment.

"Yes," I answered.

"We sure are gonna miss her here cause she is such a good neighbor, she is. Yep, she's a real nice lady. It's too bad she has to go. You know so much has changed around here. Seems like it all started with that super highway they put in and all. So, you're helping your mom move? Uh, I saw you from the window and thought you looked familiar. Didn't I go to high school with you or something?"

I was a bit perplexed. My mother wasn't such a nice lady at all, so I frowned, resisting the urge to touch my face again. "No, it wasn't me; you're thinking of my older sisters. Must have been Dena Kay who went to school with you. She was *ten* years older than me."

"Oh, yeah, Dena Dunstan. That's right. I remember now and your other sister Beth Ann. Oh man, you were that little girl, right?"

"That was me, the little girl," I answered.

"So what was it that happened to Dena?"

"She died . . . in an accident," I stammered.

"Oh, yes. I remember now. I'm sorry," he said. He stared out beyond the street into the open field with a distant look in his eyes. My eyes followed his, and I strained vainly in an attempt to see the same ghosts he saw out there.

"You know . . . I used to have a band back in those days." He mumbled, halfway to himself and halfway to me, and scraped his foot absently across the pavement.

"You know, I drove my mother crazy. She used to say to me, 'Ernesto . . . you go in that room, you listen to that Jimi Hendrix, then you turn up that Lord Zepplin, you come out and you're crazy. Can't even talk to you, ha ha.'"

"Always a rock 'n' roller. That's me. Back in the day, all right. It was something. My band played here and in Dallas and then, you know, we went and hung out in LA for a while. Yeah man, we opened for the best bands, you know . . . Santana and Steppenwolf . . . They were great . . . and all those fine ladies . . . good music . . . No, the best music!" He trailed off into the distance.

"Yes," I answered.

I did remember. Ernesto, uhh Big Daddy for short, had created his own world right here out of these millions of grains of sand, and he had taken those hopes away, only to come back. I looked far away into the distance of time when I was that skinny little kid and I could still see a banner flapping furiously against a high West Texas wind like it was yesterday there in front of that aqua painted dance hall:

BIG DADDY

AND

THE DIRTY RATFINKS

TONIGHT!

It was an image like many others: the color of the 1960s forever seared into the senses of my brain.

"Well, I was Big Daddio . . . or Big Daddy, it just depends. I like to mix it up, you know," he said, tilting his head at me.

"What? Oh . . . yeah . . . I know." I smiled.

And I did. I knew exactly what he was talking about. Those were sunshine-lollipop years, a decade of swirling, vibrant color when the world was younger and we were, too. My sisters were both at home, driving around in cars, talking to boys and drinking Coca Cola out of those itty-bitty bottles at the drive-in movie, the corner grocery, the Dairy Treat. While that world was vivid and colorful, I have remnants of it captured in black and white photographs that don't quite do it justice. It doesn't underscore my role, always tagging along with my sisters, causing a little trouble here and there. In fact, I would have to say it was a glorious time.

Maybe these moments appeal to me as a reminder of a time when I had grandparents, parents, sisters, and cousins, not to mention an added bonus of aunts and uncles.

Maybe it is this familial foundation so solidly built into that sandy soil where the spirits of my great-grandparents rose up and danced in the wind and then came softly back to earth that binds us together in a sense of continuity.

In a small, dusty rural area, there are histories and stories that should be told; times worth remembering, and there is homage, a tribute that should be paid: take the sand, all of it, mold it into castles shaped by the wind and baked by the sun. The Sandman whispers.

3 The Super Sixties

Let me introduce myself. My real name is Belinda Josephine. That was too much of a mouthful when I was something like two feet tall, so I was nicknamed Billie Jo. Beth Ann, my older sister, didn't like the name given to me by my mother, nor did she like "Billie Jo," so she gave me another nickname: "Binky." I think she had found that imprinted on a pacifier or some other baby thingy-toy. Therefore, Binky I was. Like forever. Years later I pondered the consequences of being an old woman and someone calling out "BINKY!" as I trotted along the sidewalk with my cane. Then most likely I would turn, stare at the person, if I could still see, and shake my cane at them.

During the Binky days, I had a tricycle; I was about three years old. It was bright, shiny red and ready to go. Sidewalks were longer than they are now, and many more paths ran alongside them. On a sidewalk in those days, you could travel from city to city or make your own parking lot. I was blessed with the gift of imagination, which, let me tell you, in this part of the country is a darn good thing. Armed with this gift, I could spend all day going to the post office, the grocery store, and the laundromat: places I found worth going to. I never thought where the sidewalk or the highway might end, or that they would even leave Kahler County, Texas. I did learn eventually that they did indeed go beyond that, and as I was to find out much later, this was both good and bad in many ways.

☆   ☆   ☆

My mother was known as Mama Fern. She had a knack for cleaning. In fact, she redefined the chore. Clorox bleach was an all-important part of her many daily rituals. One day in particular, she had been cleaning, and everything smelled like fresh Pine-Sol or the all-favorite bleach. Take your pick. The little black and white television was on in the corner. After her marathon cleaning, my mother was sitting on the edge of the chair, completely absorbed in it. The TV showed a bunch of cars moving and people ducking down. The newsman kept coming on and talking. It showed the pretty lady who was always on TV. She wore nice hats and gloves, but she was sad. It was 1963. A day that I later learned would define history and leave an imprint upon all our lives. My sisters came home from school, and they were sad, too. I didn't get to watch *Mr. Magoo* that day. It took years for me to understand and appreciate Dion's "Abraham, Martin and John."

☆　☆　☆

The rooster outside my bedroom crowed early in the mornings and sometimes woke me up. I could hear him from my bed when the first glimmer of sunlight came through the curtains. I had to momentarily think if I was at Mama Fern's house in town or my grandparents' farm in the country. I would grab the bed covers and run my hand over them and take a breath. If I smelled freshly bleached white cotton sheets, I was at my mother's, and if it was a chunky piece quilt with a smell of a million yesterdays sewn into it, I was at Nanny's house.

The rooster in the backyard at Mama Fern's house had been given to me by my granddad. "Merlin" was an Easter present all painted up and small. He was feisty; I liked him at once.

"Cluck, cluck!" I'd call out to him, and he would come.

The trouble was, Merlin got bigger, and as he got bigger, he became quite mean. That rooster was full-grown practically overnight, and during that time, he developed a personality disorder. He began chasing me all over the yard. Then he decided to branch out and chase Dena Kay, too. But heaven forbid! He was even brave enough to chase my mother and cause her to lose her head scarf in the bushes. When you made Mama Fern mad, you had to pay for it.

In spite of his mild psychosis and pure meanness, Merlin grew even more beautiful. His colors suddenly turned intense, as though he was truly a hand-painted object after all. Merlin looked like he had stepped out of some kind of Norman Rockwell painting—for the sole purpose of terrorizing me. The downside was that he had a quick beak and knew how to use it. His pursuit of Dena and me around the backyard and his occasional bout with Mama Fern and her scarves proved he wasn't afraid of anything, not even Mr. Ross' German shepherd dog next door. All this squabble led to a visit to my grandparents' farm.

My granddad came and picked him up one day. Caught him out there with those big, brown hands of his and put him in a big box. I think he gave him away to another farmer. I was glad to see him go. Not long after the rooster of torment left us, my granny made the best barbecued chicken I had ever tasted. I contemplated chickens both for nurturing and maybe eating.

4 Granddad

My granddad's ancestors came from Scotland. I have pictures of his grandparents stuck in my picture album. Horace Dunbar was Granddad's grandfather's name. Try saying that really fast. In a photograph I have, my great-great-grandpa looks to have been small and serious. Not only that, but he sorta resembled a leprechaun, albeit, still a serious one. Or maybe he looked like a Quaker. I can't really decide. Horace had fought in the Civil War, mainly to earn some money. He made his way as a young man to Linn County, Iowa where he got some land in the westward movement. After bustling about on the Great Frontier, Horace decided Arkansas was the place to be. He then traded all his land, sight unseen, for land in

Arkansas, climbed on a boat, and made his way down the Mississippi River to a new life.

When he arrived in Arkansas, Horace must have felt duped: as far as he could see, he gazed upon the most unfit land ever made for farming—which was a long way in this flatland. He had bought some hogs along the way and brought them with him. With the first glimpse of his new home, Horace's heart sank. The hogs were happy because when they were released on that wild, craggy land, they instantly heeded the call of the wild and became one with their ancestors: running, grunting, acting like genuine pigs, and taking up with the wild hogs already inhabiting the place. So, the domesticated pigs and the wild ones vanished together into the great Arkansas wilderness along with their primordial ancestors.

I have always wondered if Horace even tried to chase those hogs, to coral them, or to beg their pardon and their compliance to adjust to the land and act like livestock. Dad gum it! I very much doubt he attempted to address the hogs. This was way before the Horse Whisperer. Horace, the good Scotsman he was, most likely drowned his sorrows in some type of homemade brew and threw his luck to Providence. He set out to see what else he might find in the great land of Arkansas.

Part of my great-great-grandpa's fortunate new beginning came when he married the daughter of a highly successful planter. That would definitely help a person get at least one rung up on the great ladder of life. My great-great-granny's name was Harriet Ann Bagley. She had one leg that was shorter than the other; there's a name for that condition, but right now it slips my mind. Now, don't think that this handicap might have hindered her one bit. She managed a farm and a houseful of kids all on her own for many years.

I glance at her picture now, and she is wearing a scarf about her head, not one like Mama Fern's, mind you, a sorta flour sack something. Harriet's eyes are deep, her nose is large, and her jaw is square and solidly set. In that tintype, you can tell this is a capable woman. Why shouldn't she be? After all, as I picture her out on her front porch, I can see true grit: she had Yankees coming down on one side of her and Indians on the other. In my mind's eye, I imagine she was quite good with a rifle.

My granddad didn't resemble his grandparents; he was a big man whereas they were small. He had the biggest hands you ever did see. His hands shook, and I never knew why until I grew up and discovered his illnesses. My little terrier dog, Cheetah, would mimic Granddad's shaking hands by standing up on her hind legs, crossing her front paws, and moving them up and down. She did this for food, especially on cheeseburger night since she loved little pieces of meat with melted cheese. Granddad also had big, brown, milk-cow eyes that reflected the kindness in his soul. He loved all his grandchildren dearly. You can tell that by looking back at all the old pictures. He is so oblivious to the camera. He just stands there, doting on all of us and looking happy about it. My granddad would have been happy to have had a million grandkids, but he only had five of us because all the children he ever had were his two sons.

The two boys were born slightly less than a year apart, in the early twenties. This made them almost like twins, but harder to take care of. When World War II came, my granddad took the older one to Hashford to sign up to fight for the country. He told the Navy recruiter that he only had two sons in the whole wide world but he understood what needed to be done. He knew the world was turning upside down, and he was entrusting this one to them. "This one" survived the war but was waylaid down the long road of life. That, of course, is just one of life's little ironies.

Some people might hear about my granddad and say he was nothing but a dirt farmer. The fact is, he got tired of that sandy dirt pretty darned fast. Looking back at him now, he was an emblem of his time, an example of a true American with a work ethic and principles for life. After a few years of working with that impossible soil, he directed his energy toward livestock, although more so cows than those incorrigible hogs. He would hitch up his big cattle trailer to his old blue car one Saturday a month and go to the livestock sale in Hashford, Texas. Many times I would go with him because I enjoyed standing on the rails and watching the horses and cows being herded into the pens.

At the livestock auction, people could buy everything: cows, pigs, sheep, and bulls. I went with Granddad to the sale and stood on that iron fence and watched all the animals come into the arenas, wondering which ones we would take home. Thinking back, I wonder how Granddad's beat-up car could pull that trailer with one of those big cows in it. Maybe the trailer wasn't that big after all. Probably another one of those instances where things seem much bigger when you are little.

I went with Granddad all over Hashford and Kahler counties in the little, blue Ford. He took me to the Dairy Mart in Kahler City and bought me corn dogs and cokes.

Those were the best corn dogs I ever ate, as a matter of fact. When we went to town in Rockville, he would buy me tons of cokes and Baby Ruth bars. Every time I eat a Baby Ruth and drink Coca-Cola now, I am back there, say about 1966, and I'm the star of his universe in the great state of Texas, long before we talked about seceding from the United States . . . well, the Tea Party anyway.

☆   ☆   ☆

I also have a picture of Granddad with his mule. The plow is all hooked up, and my nanny is standing in front of the mule holding his reins. It's the 1920s. She's so young I can't even imagine her. It's kinda funny and rather weird looking at her in a 1920s dress and bobbed hair. I wonder what she was thinking there at that time. They are on a little isolated farm out in the country trying to get the land to give it up and make a living. She doesn't look sad or lonely at all, but I wonder how she could not be, given the circumstances and the fact she is all alone out there without her sisters or anyone else for company. Sometimes I think if the farmhouse were still there, a person could hear echoes of Granddad's footprints in the evening, that wonderful hour of dusk when the shadows creep in and the coyotes come out. Every evening after supper, Granddad made his way across the kitchen floor and through the living room to sit in his easy chair, smoke his pipe, and listen to his radio. It was a much-needed respite at the end of a long day, a time when Granddad could still his shaky hands and sit his big, lanky body down and away from the daily demands of the sweltering sun.

5 Not the Last Picture Show . . . the ONLY Picture Show

Beth Ann bounced down the steps of the front porch and tossed her small white handbag into the car where Dena and I waited. I liked watching my sister and her big hair as she adjusted it just so in the mirror. "All right, Billie Jo, you gonna be good tonight for us?" she asked.

I nodded quietly. I was always good for them.

"Yeah, right," said Dena glancing in the back seat where I sat with my clean cotton shorts and matching shirt.

"I don't go looking for trouble," I retorted, "and I don't even care if you talk to boys or not; I'm not gonna tell." The radio blared an old Buddy Holly song about a girl named Peggy Sue and how you, too, would recognize her if you saw her. I liked that song, so I decided to listen and gaze out at the serene farmland on the way to the drive-in movie, always expecting to see space aliens or specters landing on the vast horizon. The drive-in movie was the place to be. Not only was the screen bigger than a house, the speakers that fit on the windows were cool, too. And then there was the snack bar where the smell of the buttered popcorn could melt you down even before you ever got inside.

Sometimes, if the movie was just really bad or my sisters were more into socializing, I would go to the playground right outside the snack bar. There I could swing high against the night sky and cinematography and pretend I was in another world, or I could continue to look for aliens without any rude interruption.

The drive-in movie was nestled deep in prime West Texas grazing land where the only neighbors were cows. They didn't mind the intrusion into their space at all; in fact, they would oftentimes come up close to the fence and look for themselves. Maybe they were watching the movie or maybe just people watching: chew, chew, pause, think, chew, pause, watch. It must have been fun being a cow and observing the trendy movie going public right in your own backyard.

The radio music had changed and now "Georgie Girl" rang from the speakers. I tried to whistle like that British guy who sang it. I could picture Georgie, wandering around and window shopping in London. I figured that Georgie Girl would look a lot like That Girl, her hair in the same flip, but I decided her hair should be light brown. She would be just so chipper in her short plaid skirt and her hair shellacked in glistening thick hair spray. She skipped along casting flirty glances at long-haired boys who probably all looked and sounded like the Beatles.

"Okay, Billie Jo," Beth Ann was saying to me, "I'm giving you just this much money for tonight, and that's it. Do you understand?"

"Well, how much popcorn and candy can I get for that?" I asked.

"Enough to rot the rest of your teeth," quipped Dena.

I didn't like Dena Kay nearly as much as Beth Ann, at least at that time.

"Well, you certainly don't need any, so maybe I can have yours, too!" I said.

She glared back at me. "That's enough, you two," said Beth Ann. We pulled into the line for tickets. Beth Ann had told me beforehand that it was Phyllis Diller. I liked the long cigarettes she smoked and her pink feathered clothes, so this suited me just fine, or so I thought.

"I'm bored," I said to Dena Kay ten minutes into the Phyllis Diller movie.

I was, too, although it was kinda funny watching Phyllis stumble around, overfill her bubble bath, and chase that snooping little man around all over the movie screen right in the middle of a West Texas pasture.

"Be quiet," said Dena.

"Where'd Beth Ann go?" I asked.

"Right there," said Dena.

I knew where she was; she was sitting on top of the car next to us with some of her friends. I looked over at the group of teenagers. It was beyond me. I couldn't understand why they were so giggly and stupid. Then I remembered the snacks, and at that very moment, I decided to make a run for the snack bar.

"Don't be acting up out there. I don't want to have to come and get you," said Dena.

I scrunched my nose and got out of the car.

"Don't eat too much sugar and get sick," Beth Ann called out to me. I walked through the maze of cars, which seemed like hundreds at the time: all colors and sizes, all kinds of people, people you could see and those whom you couldn't, empty cars, couples kissing in cars, people standing on cars, people bored with Phyllis Diller, and probably a lot of hungry kids bored with everything, and getting out to go to the snack bar, too.

I went in and bought a small Coke and Baby Ruth bar and went outside to the swings. Lo and behold, there was Eddie Logan from school, sitting on a swing. Too late. He had already spotted me.

"Billie Jo, you here, too?" he asked.

"Yes," I said. I didn't know about him. Sometimes at school he wasn't all that nice to me, so I wasn't sure if he wanted to pick on me or not.

"I'm with my brother," said Eddie. "He's talking to some girl. Yuck."

"Yeah," I said. "Teenagers are kinda stupid sometimes."

But I noticed that Eddie himself wasn't too repulsive tonight. Sitting in that swing, he looked almost . . . well, sorta cute or something.

"Hey, you can come swing with me. This is a neat spot right here, and we can see the movie screen real good," he said. I noticed Eddie had nice hair. For a boy, he wasn't that bad. For that one night, Eddie Logan wasn't so obnoxious.

We played on the swings with the movie illuminating the landscape—Phyllis Diller, pink and all. I decided that maybe when Eddie was older, he wouldn't be such a pathetic teenager. He made faces like the ones on the screen. He told knock knock jokes.

"Knock, knock!"

"Who's there?"

"Do ya have Prince Albert in a can?"

"Yes."

"You'd better let 'em out! Ha!"

"Knock, knock!"

"Who's there?"

"Is your refrigerator running?"

"Yes."

"You'd better catch it then!"

Hmm . . . I wondered if I would ever be as funny as Eddie Logan. He was almost as funny as Johnny Carson.

"Do you like your brother?" I asked.

"Sometimes . . . it's kinda nice to go around with him in the car and all."

"And I'll bet he's always nice to you if you don't tell on him."

"Yeah, it kinda works like that." His brother whistled from a distance. "Ah man . . . well, I gotta go now. We have to be home early. See ya at school Monday."

"Sure thing, Eddie. Goodbye." I wondered if he would REALLY be that nice at school the next week or if I would just be the pesky, younger, skinny girl they made fun of over and over again.

I decided to let Eddie go out well ahead of me in case anybody tried to tease me or anything stupid like that. I went back inside and got a small popcorn for the road. I made my way back to the car amid the darkness and the ghoulish light flickering from the screen. I walked down a row of cars and studied each one . . . not it, not it, not it. *Hmmm* . . .

I opened the back door and was starting to get inside when I noticed several pairs of eyes staring back at me. I screamed. I couldn't help it. Wrong car. I had heard what happens to little girls when they get into a car full of strangers—courtesy of Aunt Millie and Dena Kay. I ran, throwing the popcorn into the air like confetti. My heart was in my throat. I ran some more. Then I heard Beth Ann laugh.

"Hey, Billie Jo, you see a ghost?" she asked.

"Uh, no . . . " I said. I knew if I told them what happened that Dena Kay would make fun of me for weeks to come, so I decided not to.

"What's wrong then?" asked Beth Ann.

"Nothing . . . aww . . . errrr . . . I was afraid I might be late," I said.

The nerdy boy on her left looked down at me and winked. *Eww!!!* I thought, totally disgusted.

6 My Best Dog

I had a Collie dog named Beau. He was beautiful—long, silky fur and skinny, cat-collie legs. My daddy joked that Beau was smarter than most of our neighbors cause he really was. Beau and I would run out into the fields and play ball in the wild flowers. My nanny even liked him. He chased squirrels and rabbits and taught me how important dogs were to human beings. Beau slept on the front porch, and together we would listen to the coyotes howling deep into the night. I thought he would always keep me safe and I would return the favor.

Myrna Turner lived down the road from us. She had a Collie dog, too. It wasn't as pretty as Beau. My nanny never liked Myrna; she thought she was a busybody.

Nanny was never one to insult anyone openly since she was all full of good Southern manners and all, but she didn't like Myrna and referred to her as "that Heifer." The fact was, "Heifer" was as strong a word as Nanny every used. Myrna didn't like my Beau. I think she was jealous, and Beau could easily get the best of her dog.

One day I went out to play. I called for Beau, but he didn't come. I wasn't worried for a while—and then I just felt something wasn't naturally right; sure thing, it wasn't. Beau did come home, almost crawling and bleeding at the mouth. My daddy saw him first. He intercepted him and took him out to the cow trough. I was looking out the kitchen window, and I knew right away. I could see his silky, cream blue fur lying by the pond.

"Billie, sweetie, don't go out there," Nanny called after me. But I had to. My daddy looked at me with sadness in his blue eyes and shook his head. I stood there with him and watched my best friend on earth take his last breath.

I learned a valuable lesson that hot, sandy summer in Texas. I learned that life isn't always fair. Sometimes you do lose something you can never have again; you miss love when it leaves you. Then that meanness and hatred reaches in with its raking, knobby hands—all the way over to puncture supreme happiness and end the perfect world of childhood.

7 Dena Has a Boyfriend

Gerald P. Loveton had a Ford Mustang that was bright red with white seats. It was a car that screamed "I. AM. MR. IT." He wore dark sunglasses and colorful clothes. Gerald had neatly trimmed hair; he closely resembled one of the Beach Boys. In fact, I thought Gerald stepped out of the "Fun, Fun, Fun" song. I wondered if there was a song written about taking a Mustang away from a boy like the one where the T-bird was taken away from the girl.

I don't remember many of my sisters' other boyfriends, but I certainly do remember Gerald pulling up in front of my Grandmother Lola's house to pick up Dena Kay. She wore one of those skirts that she couldn't wear to high school. The skirts she wore to school had to be measured so that they would still touch the floor when the girls kneeled. No, this skirt was short all right.

I even liked the sound of Gerald's name ... LOVETON. What kind of name was that?

"A Groovy Kind of Love ..." blared from his radio. I just stood there and watched him open the door for Dena. I would kinda like to have had a ride in that car myself. As far as the dating business, I still didn't know what all the fuss was about, and I wondered if I would ever be climbing into a Mustang with Eddie Logan. I decided NO WAY and went back inside to finish watching *That Girl* and to ponder bigger issues in the world: should I be a teacher ... or a twirler. After all, twirling a fire baton in Texas without catching one's clothes on fire is an art.

8 | Nanny

I called my paternal grandmother "Nanny." She was probably one of my most favorite people on the planet. By the time I was born, all my grandparents were already into their sixties, so they were older and nicer than most other adults. Nanny was Scots-Irish. Her fifth great-grandfather was a man by the name of David Garvin. David and his wife Elizabeth were Scottish and belonged to a religion known as Covenanters.

In the 1600s, religious turmoil ran amuck in Scotland, like werewolves, and it just wasn't a good time to practice Covenanting, so they fled during the period known as the "Killing Time." The David Garvin family arrived in Londonderry, Ireland to pick up their lives and start anew with their two boys. Eventually, after a couple of generations passed, Thomas Garvin, the grandson of David, came to America and settled in Pennsylvania before moving on to the South. In a nutshell, that is how my nanny ended up with her wonderful Celtic features, the red golden hair she had when she was younger, her thin frame, and a fabulous sense of humor.

My nanny loved her only two boys. She had a rough time when my daddy was born: he was a sick baby. The doctor didn't think he would live. Nanny decided right then and there in that West Texas sand, under that omnipotent sun, and against the howling wind, that my daddy would indeed live. She watched him twenty-four hours a day. She wouldn't let herself sleep at night. When she dozed off, she would stick her fingers with a needle to keep herself awake. Nanny spent half the night sobbing and the other half praying that her baby wouldn't die. Her efforts paid off. The strong Texas woman won that battle.

My Uncle Dail was only about a year younger than my daddy. When he first ran off as a young man and joined the Navy, my nanny wrote to her mother-in-law about how the Navy took a kid who was too young to go. She talked about how my granddad was trying to get him out of the Navy, and she said with resilience that our government was the "biggest liar I ever heard." After all, it wasn't a good time during World War II to have not only one son but two out there in that crazy world. The Floodgates of Hell were letting loose. It wasn't a time to let go, at least before you had too anyway, and Nanny knew as well as anyone that both her blue-eyed boys were bound to go, as they did, albeit a couple of years later.

It was hard for Nanny when she lost her youngest son. The war didn't take him even though these were the odds back then. Instead, a car accident ended his young life, and that is where the irony comes in. Unlike my father, who pretty much rode about on a ship stateside, my Uncle Dail made several forays to Europe. During leave time in the "war to end tyranny," Uncle Dail was visiting a friend in Del Rio, Texas where he retrieved his car to drive home. On the way, he picked up a hitchhiker. This was more common in those days than during the '70s when all those slasher movies like the *Texas Chainsaw Massacre* were made. Somehow something went terribly wrong on a long, winding road with steep ditches. Uncle Dail lost control of his car, and he and the hitchhiker went over the edge. Uncle Dail never regained consciousness, and he succumbed to a head injury while the drifter was able to climb right out of the crumpled car and keep going after the police had finished questioning him.

I never knew my uncle, but I looked through some pictures of him when I was a little girl. Something about his quirky smile and his brilliant blue eyes made me want to know more about him. I looked at the pictures of his funeral. Nanny had stuffed them into a small box in her bureau. The photos had a yellow tint to them, like the setting of a late afternoon sun. Against the backdrop of the cemetery, I saw uniformed military men in the photographs holding the flag, and I saw his coffin, shiny and black. The mourners were lined up around it, and there were big, bright cars, the essence of vehicles of the flirtatious fifties.

The last shots are of the funeral director standing in front of the gravesite which was covered in red, yellow, and white flowers. Some of the Navy boys folded up the flag right properly. The entire scene screams of sadness, sorrow, and permanence. I can only imagine how my sweet, frail nanny felt on the day they buried her youngest son. So, there they lay him to rest in the quiet of the dry land, forever more to spend eternity as a young man in uniform who finally came home to stay.

From time to time, Nanny and I went to the cemetery to visit his grave. It was always fascinating to me that a person could die so young and handsome. Nanny had one of Uncle Dail's Navy pictures encased in the headstone. Sometime after that picture was put on the marker, vandals came into the cemetery and scratched through his right eye. I hated the abject lack of sensitivity of mean people. I couldn't imagine anyone so terrible that they would want to mar such a precious face, a face full of such brightness and hope.

As recompense for losing Uncle Dail, Nanny got me. That was such a bonus, but at least I kept her from being lonely. She thought most everything I did was all right. She didn't mind my endless mud pie making, and I never got too dirty at all on the farm, unlike at my mother's house where Mama Fern complained of my constant messes. Nanny told me lots of stories about her family: how her pa, Stephen Christopher Garvin, had come from Georgia and settled in Texas. How they had a covered wagon before cars came out and before people could actually afford one.

Nanny told me about the time they were coming home from church one night in the wagon.

The dirt roads were carved roughly out of the sandy soil and made small pathways to the little corners of the community. It was a relatively calm, clear West Texas night, and the moon was full and the sky lit with a million stars. It was quiet in the wagon since the girls were tired after church service and the morning chores came early. As Papa Garvin was driving the team of horses along, they started acting up, appearing jumpy, not wanting to go forward. He tried vainly to stare into the distance at something beneath the trees. Nothing appeared ahead of them, so he urged the horses forward. As the reluctant horses went forward, Papa Garvin soon discovered his folly: there in the calm, moonlit night, perched on a giant tree branch, was a large black cougar that let out a powerful, bloodcurdling scream as he contemplated his strike.

The Garvin girls froze. Time took a weird turn. Large green eyes glowed glistening, menacing gold. Fate hung in the balance while the hands of some Scottish deities of eternity, or possibly a host of Methodist prayers already uttered, seemingly decided whether that cat would attack and where their own destiny would lie after this night. Papa Garvin looked up and met the big cat's gaze. He raised his whip, halfway to show the animal he would fight and halfway to give the horses the command to run full speed. Luck held. The cougar didn't strike, and the horses flew down the small dirt path. The girls could still hear his screams in the distance. That one night stood out in Nanny's memory as almost a life-altering event, and it stuck with her from the time she was a young girl.

☆　☆　☆

Nanny had five sisters: she was the second daughter. Times could be rough on a Texas farm, especially when a farmer didn't have any sons to help take the plow, but Stephen Garvin loved his girls, curls and all. One day at breakfast, Nanny was sitting beside her next younger sister, Naomi. The table was long, and the girls sat lined up on wooden benches next to the table. Nanny's mother asked Naomi to please pass the oatmeal. She picked the bowl up from the table to hand it across, when quite suddenly, the bowl began to turn in her hand and spill over the sides onto the table.

"Oh, Naomi, don't spill it, please!" said Nanny's mother. CRASH!! The bowl went down to meet the table and Naomi slipped from the bench and onto the floor. At first, Nanny thought she was caught in something that was lasting forever, frozen in time. The white dresses swirled, and everybody was on the floor trying to raise Naomi off the hard floor. Nanny's eight-year-old sister had had a fatal stroke. It was the end for her. Part of the Garvin girls was forever gone now. They would no longer entwine arms and walk down the dirt path, huddle up together in rain storms, or help their mother do chores with Naomi.

These tragedies were quite common to the folks who settled the rolling plains: the cycles of fear, death, doubt, and hard work. But these are the people who established West Texas and enriched the land and the lives of those of us who came after, by the grace of God.

9 Ernesto Goes to Sunny California

"It Never Rains in Southern California . . . " What a funny song; I once thought, but what a good idea at the same time. For sunny California was the place of dreams, cool cars, beaches, pretty people, and the place where Ernesto was chasing dreams on Santana's guitar strings. The club scene was going strong in LA: hipsters and what would finally become the "ME" generation. It was a time of protest and resentment, of politics and questioning, but Lord, what a time for music.

Ernesto ran up and down Sunset Strip and stopped into clubs like The Bourbon Club where you could see SOMEBODY and maybe even get to talk to them, too. There were the Coconut Sea Grotto, Showgirls Rock

Sunset, the Fancy Guest Room, and Oh Babee Doll—
so many places to go and be seen. California was much
better than Texas, especially better than that little dirt spot
where Ernesto, um . . . Big Daddy grew up. Not only that,
there were movie stars on the Sunset Strip. Girls with big
hair. Ernesto hadn't seen any stars, but he just knew he
would soon. Who knew, maybe a slinky starlet in a cat
suit just like Cat Woman?

Aside from worrying about his mother, things were
good. Life could be a party, and music was his life.
Ernesto learned to play more than just the three chords
of the guitar, despite knowing some bands that did okay
with so few. However, he never could find the sounds
that the man Santana could turn out, even though it was
still a while before he premiered at Woodstock to show
the world what he could do with music . . . that certain
haunting Latino sound.

Ernesto was gonna give that music thing a try anyway.
He was heading over to his bass player's house, hoping
Roger's girlfriend wasn't home. Janey was a mean woman
and pretty large, too, while Roger was rather small. Loud,
but really small. Actually, Janey was about the size of
a small tank. Sometimes she would get mad at Roger.
Roger had told him about an incident when Janey got so
mad that she did some major property damage: she ran
through a wall to get to him.

"No kidding?" asked Ernesto incredulously.

"It's true," said Roger.

"How did she do that?"

"She's strong. She was just sitting there one minute,
and next thing I know, she was blasting through the wall,
sheetrock and all."

"But aren't there studs and things in a wall?" asked Ernesto who remembered his failed days of workshop in high school.

"Dude, I don't know the anatomy of a wall. She just ran through the whole damn thing."

"Man," said Ernesto shaking his head. He was glad he always went for the skinny bikini, cat suit types.

10 Driving Around with Beth Ann

It was hot in July, actually an understatement for Texas. What did air-conditioning mean on a farm in 1966? Well, at least, what did it mean to my granddad who was still living a bit behind the times? Not much. I'm not sure he had even heard of it. We didn't have one in the house or the blue Ford.

It was on one of these days when we jumped into the Ford and went for a cold drink at the nearest drinking place on the county line. In Texas, people sure are thirsty. The Joint was, after all, one of the few places to go, and I liked having somewhere to go. At the drinking place, they had big blocks of ice that they brought from the ice house, plus they had air conditioning and more Baby Ruth bars than a person could count.

On this particular day, Beth Ann and I had Coca-Colas and peanuts, not mixed into the bottles like the old men downtown had when they got together for dominoes. You know what they did? Ate the peanuts and then drank the Coke, or stuffed the peanuts into the coke bottle.

Beth Ann kept looking at herself in the car mirror. She had a new thing she was trying out. She was into ironing her hair. I almost can't blame her; I had never seen hair as curly as hers. My hair wouldn't even curl on those little spongy, pink rollers, but Beth Ann's hair was naturally kinky curly. I examined her meticulously ironed locks carefully in that most expert July sun.

"Beth Ann, I don't think I'm gonna have to iron my hair," I said.

"Nope," she said, eyeing me at an angle. "Your hair is perfectly straight already."

"So how'd I get straight hair, and how'd you get really curly hair, and why does Dena Kay have sorta curly hair?" I asked.

"*Hmmm*, don't know . . . maybe the milkman?" said Beth Ann.

"What'd ya mean, the milkman? Did I drink the wrong kind of milk?" I asked.

Beth Ann laughed. "No. Just a joke. Sometimes that can happen and people in the same family just don't look alike. They can take after different people who are long gone."

"Like an ancestor?" I asked. I was proud that I remembered the word from somewhere. "What's that mean, anyway—'ancestor'?"

"Silly, it's your great-grandmother, and her mother and father and their mothers and fathers and on and on and on and on . . . " she said.

"Oh, right," I said.

I reflected on this. Our mother had dark, curly hair, and she was short, too.

"I certainly don't look like Mama Fern."

"No, you don't," said Beth Ann. "I think you probably look a lot like the flower girl . . . you know the one somewhere in California where the guy says she had made him happy with all the flowers in her hair." Beth Ann winked at me, and we just had to sing it:

"I knew, I knew, I knew, I knew she would made me HAPPEE . . . flowers in the air!"

I wondered about that, too, because my hair was so fine and all, the flowers would probably just slide right on out, and I wouldn't look good in California dancing around without flowers sticking all over me.

☆   ☆   ☆

The next best state to California was probably Arizona; after all, they were pretty close together out there. We had cousins who lived there and they would often visit, bringing civilization to our little corner of the world. Beth Ann was especially close to them and had gone to Arizona for a visit. They had introduced her to snipe hunting by hauling her out into the middle of the desert and leaving her with a burlap sack and instructions to scoop up the snipe when they chased it toward her.

"They like to hide, so they'll just run into the sack by themselves," said the cousins.

Personally, I would have tremendous misgivings sacking up some creature I had never seen before. A snipe probably looked like heaven-knows-what, perhaps a bloodsucking monster, or maybe a wolverine. I wondered where Beth Ann's normal sense of intelligence was when she decided to tackle this in the middle of the night with all those horrible night creatures lurking about and without even knowing what a snipe was or how many teeth they had. This is exactly how all of us Texans get a bad reputation for being gullible.

We had two cousins who were about Beth Ann's age. They would take turns visiting us on the farm in the summer. Though there were not many snipes running loose on my granddad's farm, the cousins all gathered in Beth's room with her friends. I lost my spot in the blue Ford. When they were around, I was relegated to solitude in the swing where I would have to reflect on their funny accents and their insistence on calling colas "pops" and calling everyone else "you guys" when I didn't even look anything like a boy. Well, except for that time when Beth Ann was in her Twiggy phase and had all my hair cut off in a pixie cut in second grade. I definitely looked like a boy then, plus my hair was a little crooked and uneven, making me look more like an evil elf. I also contemplated snakes. I wondered whether Arizona had larger rattlesnakes or whether Texas snakes were bigger. Then I had to wonder which ones made the loudest sounds, Arizona or Texas snakes? I was going to have to remember to ask Beth Ann if she had heard any rattlesnakes in the Arizona desert when she was hunting snipes.

11 Arizona . . . Put on Your Rainbow Shoes

My least favorite cousin was Henrietta. We called her "Hank" for short. Hank mostly hung around Dena Kay when she came to stay with us for the summers. Although you couldn't tell by the name, Hank was a goddess, and I do mean a bona fide goddess of the preternatural beauty sort. She could have been Venus herself.

Hank was a Muse, born to inspire men to poetry, irrational excitement, and a desire to soar to greater heights. I can shut my eyes right now and see her walking down the path leading to the farm house. Her red, wavy hair captures glints of sunlight which bounce off it into a thousand echoes; her green eyes focus with a sort of abject melancholy; her skin is so smooth and tan she could have just hopped out of a Coppertone commercial. Then, as it must, we became older, and she reminded me of a beautiful red-haired mermaid who lured sailors to crash on rocks, falling to their death. What's more, Hank thought she was something else, too. All right, and so did most people who met her, especially if they were boys. But it didn't impress me, and besides, I just flat didn't like Hank. With her, it was "you guys this" and "you guys that," and "we don't talk like this in Arizona." "You all talk so funny here . . . what's a YAWLLLLL?"

Let's face it, folks. As far as I was concerned, there was only room for one Scottish princess in this small section of Texas earth, and I already had that nailed. You could just ask my daddy.

What made me mad? Well, let me tell you. Hank just needed to leave. She and Dena took over my tree house for starters, and they knew darn well it was my tree because I was in it most of the time. They languished in it, looked down at me, smirked, and teased. As luck would have it, that was also the summer I had my smallpox vaccination, and wouldn't you know, I had to be the one to explain to Mama Fern how the scab got knocked off when Hank and Dena Kay pushed me out of my own tree house.

I was right. Mama Fern was really mad. Dena Kay got into big trouble. The other problem was this was indeed the South. Therefore, company was company, so Princess Hank got off with no consequences. I can still see her smirking, turning up the volume on the transistor radio, and listening to her favorite song . . . "Hanky Panky." All the while tossing her red locks into the diminishing Texas sunlight along with my diminishing spirit.

We had Hank for a few weeks that summer, but it seemed forever. She met my other cousin Jesse from my mother's side of the family, and they hit it off. I didn't like the way this was going at all, even though she wasn't related to him. I was beginning to think there was a reason why folks' family trees stopped branching out, and I had to watch Jesse make a fool out of himself, which he did quite adeptly. He started showing up at weird times, unannounced, trying to stay on my good side, and then buying Hank chocolate shakes and candy bars.

Jesse was pathetic, giddy, unpredictable: the whole mess. Why couldn't he see Hank for what she was–a black widow spider dressed as a mermaid, but better looking? This new love situation wasn't a good deal for me at all. They just got in my way, and I couldn't concentrate on the larger issues of life. You can imagine my supreme happiness when the time came for Hank to pack up and head back to that sophisticated but dry, Arizona desert where people didn't drawl their words at all.

12 School Days

Sometimes in Texas you really do get hung up on a cowboy. I knew one in third grade. His name was Zane. His hair was the color of sand, but with highlights. It wasn't like Hank's or anything, but when I saw him, I thought he had really nice hair, and I sorta glowed when he walked by. His eyes were light green but sometimes brown; they seemed to change colors along with his shirt. One day he smiled at me at recess.

"Hey, wanna play pick-up sticks?" he asked shyly.

"Sure," I replied and adjusted the collar of my white turtleneck sweater. Zane had never asked girls to play pick-up sticks with him before. This must be special indeed.

"Do you ride horses?" Zane asked.

"No, we don't have any horses, just cows and pigs and chickens," I replied.

"Maybe you'd like to learn to ride a horse one day. I could teach ya," he smiled.

"Yeah, maybe so," I replied.

I was dubious about all this cowboy stuff because I had seen the ranch roundup. This was an annual event made up of honest-to-goodness cowboys. And rodeo queens, too. That was always fun watching the queens in jeans and bright colored shirts with those little, pearly snap buttons. One time there was this cowboy and some cowgirl riding ahead of him. They must have been having a disagreement because he took his lasso and roped her right off her horse. She hit the ground with a thud and ruined her shiny, yellow cowgirl shirt. Riding horses, I don't think so . . .

"Hey, you'd like my horse. Really, I think you would," said Zane.

"Oh, you know what? Something really neat happened last night," I changed the horse subject.

"What happened?" he asked.

"A bull snake got into my nanny's chicken pen," I said.

"Really?" he answered.

"And you know what? My daddy heard the chickens, and he just automatically knew what it was."

"Wow!" Zane replied.

"He went out into the chicken yard and saw the snake. It was huge. He grabbed hold of the end of it and had to wrestle it. The snake thrashed and twisted in Daddy's hands. The chickens squawked; I stared with my mouth open. Daddy frowned. Bull snake—Daddy—bull snake—Daddy. Chickens. Me. In what seemed like a rather long time, but then again, not really, my daddy won the fight, and he popped off the snake's head!"

"Oh wow! That's wild. And a big snake, too. The only snakes I ever see are rattlers because we don't have any chickens," said Zane.

I could see our class in the distance, running and giggling, and I knew there would be heck to pay with the teasing and all that. But I didn't care. I grabbed a fist full of the brightly colored sticks and let them drop.

"Yeah, the thing about those snakes is they're just pretty smart. They wait until there's no human activity outside. They survey every inch of their stakeout with glowing eyes. They sneak and crawl around the pen, sizing up the chickens. I think the bottoms of their stomachs have little feet or antennae things on them. They wait until the right moment and slither over the tin. Slime and metal. They drop smack dab into the chicken house with a loud THUD right where the hens are sitting on their eggs and the baby chickens are hatching. Then they open their mouths, so big, so wide, so terrible, and they swallow the babies and the eggs, maybe even a little banty hen if she moves slowly. The hens flee below the darkening, blood streaked sky and squawk and pray that somebody, like a strong daddy, is around to save the eggs and the little ones."

In this manner, I elaborated the story. When I came up for air, I noticed Zane was just staring at me. He looked weak, like all the blood had just drained to his feet. *Maybe he has a nervous stomach, too*, I thought.

"Uh, I think it's time to go now," he said, hurriedly picking up the sticks.

Hmmm . . . I might have been just a bit too dramatic with him, but I sure thought boys were supposed to be tough, at least that's what they tell us in Texas.

Zane didn't walk into class with me that day, but later on he did smile at me across the room. *A little weak, and a weak stomach*, I thought. Even then, I wondered where all the good cowboys had gone. Then it was time for physical education class.

I hated P.E. except when we got to play with the parachutes. Then it was okay. No such luck today: we had to change into shorts and everything. I took off my new locket that Nanny had just given to me and laid it carefully in the bottom of the locker and put it under my sweater. It looked like running time, and boy, did I ever hate running. Sharon Anders passed me on the way out of the locker room and roughly nudged me with her shoulder. I also hated Sharon, maybe even more than I hated running.

"Stop it," I said.

She smirked. "Oh . . . EXCUSE ME!" She roughly brushed my shoulder, her dark eyes flashing trouble.

"Got a boyfriend?" she asked as she tossed back a lock of braided hair.

"No, I don't."

"No, you don't . . . NOBODY likes you," she sneered.

"I don't care."

"GIRLS, what is the problem?" asked Mrs. Hinkle, the P.E. teacher.

Sharon smiled sweetly. "There is no problem at all, Mrs. Hinkle," she replied.

"How about you, Billie Jo?" she asked.

"No, ma'am. No problem at all," I replied. But I knew
. . . I knew that Evil walked the face of the earth. That
Evil wore braids and interfered with everybody's life. I
knew Sharon Anders was definitely a shade of menace.

"Good, let's get started," Mrs. Hinkle said and then
blew that hideous whistle.

Who invented running anyway? Around the school
yard once and my head was pounding. If I squinted
really hard, I could see parachutes or a dodge ball . . .
somewhere out there somebody was having fun.

Mrs. Hinkle's philosophy was that people ought to
run more and be in good shape and then people could
play basketball when they got to high school, be fast and
earn points, and keep the coach in a job cause she was a
coach, too. It was also a good way to help other people.
The people who worked as teachers helped wind down
a few noisy girls so there wouldn't be any idle chatter
going on after P.E. Other people needed to concentrate
and learn how to become even better people . . .

"Billie Jo, a word with you, please," said Mrs. Hinkle
after we had finally finished.

"Yes, ma'am," I answered.

"Billie Jo, I really expect that you will mind your
good manners better from now on and that you won't
be arguing with your classmates anymore. After all,
you have such a lovely, hardworking grandmother," Mrs.
Hinkle said to me.

"Yes, ma'am," I said.

I could feel my heart fall to my feet. I felt helpless,
like all the wind had really been sucked out of me this
time. So I went back to the locker room where I caught a

glance from Sharon in the corner. She smirked at me. I calmly ignored her and walked over to my locker to pull out my clothes. When I reached for my sweater, I first tucked my hand under to grab my locket; I couldn't feel it. I shook the sweater. Nothing. My locket was gone! My very special locket that Nanny had just given me, precious indeed by the fact that she washed and ironed other people's clothes for extra money and then spent that on me. I was sick, I was angry, and I looked Sharon Anders square in the face. I knew, and she very well knew it, too. She had taken the locket. I had no proof, and if I said anything now, I would be the one to get the brunt of the punishment. Sharon smiled at me and tucked her jacket under her arm as she walked out of the dressing room. I turned to my locker and tried so hard to quell the knot forming in my throat and the tears welling in my eyes.

13 DRAMA

It is hard being an actor in West Texas, especially when you are typecast and working with limited parts. I always wanted to be the main star, you know, the princess, the ghost, the wildly deranged witch. I never got those good, juicy roles. They always went to a more princess-type girl than what I was. Instead, I got to be the mother, the queen, the maid, the Edith Ann, basically anything dowdy. Even though I was quite alive and bursting with exuberance, it is no wonder that my acting talents became crippled and subdued in that environment.

In third grade, I was awarded the part of the mother of Tiny Tim in *A Christmas Carol*. I wasn't exactly excited. I wanted to be the GHOST OF SOMETHING, but I can well remember what I wore to the first rehearsal: a white school girl sweater and red pants. I knew that when the time came for the actual play there was no way that the poor mother would get to wear anything vibrant, like the color red, so I had to make it count while I could.

When the time came for the actual performance, Ceila Adams and I got to make announcements on the stage to all the parents and other adoring members of the crowd. Ceila and I got along real well, so I was glad to get to do this with her. The night of the play, she was so very sad because her little white poodle, Muffin, had run away, and Ceila was all whiny-like and everything.

I was the mother, Mrs. Cratchit, in the play; Jeremy Trott was Tiny Tim, and he was, as I had heard a teacher put it, "a little slow." Sometimes he would forget his lines, and I would have to hiss them through my motherly well-meaning smile as I sat across the table from him. This was before Mr. Scrooge's generosity, so it was easy to see Jeremy. The table was quite bare. I hated having a husband and all that, especially since it wasn't Zane. Instead, it was that completely irritating Steven Bower who pulled my hair and called me names. No, while I was busy being the dowdy mother that Charles Dickens had created, the love of my life got to be one of the coveted ghosts, the Ghost of Christmas Past. To make matters worse, Sharon was the Ghost of Christmas Future which the teachers embellished, plus she got to be dark and exciting in intense, black eyeliner. Meanwhile, I was having to worry about having a turkey to cook and if poor, failing Tiny Tim would make it not only through dinner but Christmas as well.

The day before the play, I fell off the monkey bars. Actually, it wasn't the one in the schoolyard—it was one I had fashioned myself with an iron bar stuck between two trees. My engineering skills had yet to kick in. In the third grade, I did not realize that the bar would begin to slip inch by inch as I swayed and jiggled and sang:

"Hey, Hey we're the Monkees . . . we're busy playing . . . DOWN!"

KERPLUNK!

Well, let me tell you, I got put down—put down in a hurry as I fell almost on top of my head. I managed to get up, even though I was a bit winded. I didn't cry. In my severe moment of pain, looking across the yard, I saw a little dog running down the sidewalk, a white poodle. Oh my goodness! *Muffin!*

I got up and managed to run after her and called her name. She turned once to look at me and then ran into somebody else's yard. I paused. Goodness! It was old, cranky Mrs. Wilson's house. I couldn't go back there because everybody said she was a witch or something. I just knew she would be boiling a kettle for Muffin. If I dared to look, she was probably already making the next batch of stew in some big, black pot beneath the trees. I felt sick to my stomach, and I pondered on the quandary of telling Ceila or not. Oh, to survive major head trauma and be worried about a small, white, defenseless poodle at the same time!

The afternoon of the play, I put on my maxi-length dress in the dressing room. These dresses were handy dandy before celebrity baby mamas began sporting them with flip flops when pregnant, or pretty much any time. The long dress relics of the past not only helped rock a crochet poncho, mood ring, or Indian headband piece but also worked quietly and conveniently as costumes for the mother role I was playing.

I waited until Ceila came in and asked, "Ceila, by chance has Muffin come home yet?"

"No," she replied sadly.

"*Hmmmm*, do you uh, ever go walking by Mrs. Wilson's house?"

"Not really, why?" she asked.

"Well, I just thought that might be a good place to look if you haven't already."

"Do you think she has Muffin?" Ceila asked.

"Well, I don't know." I stammered because I was quite worried if Mrs. Wilson was a real witch and all that. Because if she was, she might be viewing us that very minute in her cauldron or her crystal ball. You know, witches have all those accessory items and whatnots and I was truly afraid she might put a curse or spell on us . . . or something.

"I saw a little white dog and that's all. I don't really know if it was her or not," I lied.

"*Hmmm*," Ceila said and frowned. "I don't think it was Muffin. She never went that far."

"Probably not," I said frowning to myself.

Poor Muffin, I thought, *she might now be witch soup, or chicken feed, but I had work to do.* I had to put it out of my head and focus with a practically clear conscience as I transformed into Mrs. Cratchitt. I was kinda hoping they would dangle Sharon Anders from ropes when the time for her part came. It might even be possible for those ropes to break or accidentally get gnawed into by some roving beaver. Sharon might even fall from her lofty perch as the most exciting character in the play and get a little dose of what it felt like to fall out of a tree with a defective monkey bar just because she stole my locket and I felt that some type of retribution should be in order.

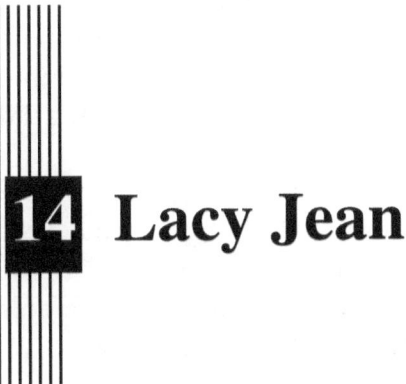

14 Lacy Jean

It's a really good thing to have cousins, and usually people who live in small towns have lots of them. It's a good thing, but it is also a reason that some of us have to grow up and leave: that way our family tree will continue to branch out and not go straight. I had lots of cousins, and there were some good times and other times were not so good. I think the one relative that fascinated me the most was Lacy Jean.

Beth Ann could not stand Lacy Jean. Oh, I think part of it was just jealously. Actually, I think most of it was jealousy. Lacy Jean was a Southern girl through and through. Plus, she was very much a girlie girl. I think she started bleaching and teasing her hair when she was thirteen. Don't even let me get started on her nails. By the time she was sixteen, Lacy Jean had a glorious patch of finely ratted, bleached blonde hair piled high on the top of her head. I did admire this feat because my hair was as fine as a baby's. I had no idea how in the world I would ever manage to get my hair to look like that whenever I got to be a teenager. So it was beginning to appear more and more like I might have to go to California and join the Mod Squad or something because Peggy Lipton did not have hair like Lacy's.

Lacy Jean knew how to talk and nod accordingly. Listening to her was sorta like listening to some slow, Southern melody complete with an "I'll swan . . . " as she surveyed the conversation behind expressive blue eyes rimmed with eyelashes like black velvet curtains.

It was interesting to watch her talk to boys. Inevitably, they would become all caught up in the conversational experience and forget what to answer back or just get caught staring at her. Sometimes they would say things that didn't make any sense. She would murmur on such topics as "Billy Ray, how is your mother doing?"

Billy Ray might turn all red and respond, "Great. We let her out of the feed lot just this morning. I mean, the cow. You know the black heifer?"

I would snicker to myself while fighting back the urge to ask him, "Billy Ray, can you talk to Lacy without staring at the daisies on her shirt?"

"Beth Ann, what's wrong with Lacy Jean?" I asked.

"She's just stupid," said Beth Ann.

"You mean she can't do math?" I asked.

"I mean she can't do math or anything else right," said Beth Ann.

"She isn't any good in school?"

"No, she even failed second grade," Beth Ann said.

"But she knows how to cook," I pointed out.

"Trust me, when she marries that Adam Thornton, she's going to need to know how to cook. She will be stranded out on that farm for the rest of her life frying chicken and baking lemon pies," said Beth Ann.

"Isn't that what a lot of people do?" I asked.

"Good grief! Not anymore! They join the WAC," said Beth Ann getting a bit irritated.

"The Wax?"

"It's the military. That's what it is—but for girls," said Beth Ann.

"Oh, all right," I said.

That was fine with me. Anything I guess but frying chickens. There was no way I could kill one or pluck its feathers. I was Fowl Impaired for sure. I saw Daddy plucking them, too. No way I could do it, and besides, I really didn't want to grow up to be a farmer's wife anyway. I wanted to grow up to be That Girl and live in New York City.

At the same time, I felt you had to admire Lacy Jean. She was the quintessential blonde, and she would certainly have everyone's vote here, especially the boys'. It was like she was from another planet or something. The God of Genetics had smiled down on her and had given the plain countryside something beautiful in its midst. She was just almost unearthly. In my dreams, all Lacy Jean needed was a pink convertible to cruise out of the drive-in pasture into a Hollywood movie where I'd just bet she wouldn't be playing the mother or the dowdy queen.

15 Peaks and Mountains

Daddy liked to go outside in the evenings when it was sorta noisy quiet and the sun was beginning to set and the night bugs had just started making their sounds. He would walk out onto the front porch and survey Kiowa Peak rising eastward in the distance. Daddy had been there and climbed it, too. Beth Ann had proudly pointed this out to me. One such semi-magical, country evening, he looked out into the distance and pondered the peak.

"Daddy carved my initials up there on a rock when I was only five years old," Beth Ann announced to me.

"Why is it called Kiowa Peak?" I asked.

"Well, it's named after one of the Indian tribes who lived here," said Beth Ann. "It's special because it has a lost copper mine on it."

"Well, that has yet to be found," replied Daddy. "I suppose it is possible. Sits right there above the Salt Fork of the Brazos; the Comanche and Apache Indians and Spanish settlers used to roam about up there."

"Peter Simmons said someone found evidence of alien visits, too." said Beth Ann.

Wow, I thought to myself. Aliens right here in West Texas. Who could beat that? Just imagine! Why would they rather be here than California or even New York? Probably because there were fewer people to spot them. What if they were coming to take Lacy Jean away because she really didn't belong here? What if they looked like little men with green skin, or big tall ones with huge heads and big black eyes? And did they wear cowboy hats on top of their little green heads and spurs on their little green ankles?

No matter, I sure bet they scared the howl right out of the coyotes up there, and probably even the ghosts of the Indians and the Spanish. "Apparently, some landmarks shifted. When they came back for it, they couldn't find it. Many people have searched for it, but nobody has found it," said Daddy. "Seems like a great deal of bad luck has happened to those folks who've looked for the treasure."

"Gee, like a curse?" I asked.

"Well, I don't really know, but let's just say nobody has ever found a treasure. Hearts have been broken, lives have been altered, and who knows, maybe some will continue to look and be disappointed," said Daddy.

"I'll bet the rattlesnakes guard the treasure, kinda like cobras do in Africa. They're probably so big and dangerous that people just can't go near it. They have all those rocks up there, too, so there're probably millions of snakes! I'll bet the snakes have those treasure rocks, and they slither and slide their greasy bodies all over them at night, and they look out upon us with their red eyes and seething venom!" I exclaimed, rather proud of myself over the image I had just created.

"Sure that must be exactly it, like there aren't snakes all over West Texas," said Beth Ann scornfully as she gave me one of her I-am-almost-a-grown-up-and-you-are-not looks.

Daddy chuckled. I could see he was amused but also lost in his own thoughts. We could tell he liked it out there as the dusk enveloped our tiny spot of the world. You know, just enjoying being lost in it by himself and all that. We all three gazed out at the peak in the distance; Daddy was quiet. I don't know what he saw out there, maybe the peak, maybe the past, maybe even episodes of World War II he had experienced. Beth Ann and I looked at each other, then tiptoed off, leaving him there to contemplate the Spanish missionaries, the Indians, and the aliens converging through space and time and hiding spider rocks around the perimeter of the peak to be discovered by unsuspecting Texans trying to make their fortunes.

16 Vampires

Dena Kay liked to take me to the movies when she didn't have anyone else to ask. I liked going; actually, I'd go about anywhere. After all, it wasn't a whole lotta fun and also rather tricky, playing dodge ball by yourself. Dena Kay just loved scary movies. She liked to watch me squirm and sometimes scream, so she took me to see *Count Yorga Vampire* at the local movie palace. That movie made a mark on my existence to say the least. Yep, there's always that one movie that reaches out to me now, well beyond the years, and the more horrific the scenes . . . the better.

At this time in my life, way before the *Twilight Saga*, I discovered just how dangerous and deceitful these vampire creatures could be. Here I had been, walking around for nearly ten years and I didn't have a clue that all of mankind was in vast danger. If only I had known, I might have been less concerned with rattlesnakes. They both had fangs, but the undead presented a whole new set of problems. Had I known, I would have taken precautions at night and gathered up some crosses and garlic and never ever would I have raised my window. I would've been especially careful about covering up my neck at dark and about sleeping completely under the covers. Because after all, nobody would want to look up and see one of those creatures staring back at you from the closet door behind your sister's old pink prom dress.

Count Yorga was crafty. By this I mean his house was way out in the boonies and all that so he could go around relatively unnoticed. In the Count's massive dining room, he had a nice big dinner table set for guests, but, of course, he had more plans in store for them. The Count liked the main character's girlfriend, Erica. You know, of course, it was because she looked like his long-lost love. After dinner, the unsuspecting guests' van had to get stuck out there in a heavily wooded area. Like those movie scenes where the girl just has to go down into the basement although all the electricity is off and the Portal of Hell is exploding down there. Plus, I doubt that unsuspecting girl in the movie knows a thing about electrical wiring and couldn't fix anything if she wanted to. Anyway, after dinner was over, the guests had to spend the night out there stranded in the woods not far from Count Yorga's mansion.

Well, I knew things weren't looking good and let me tell you that Erica, yep, she was a goner all right.

Count Yorga went out looking for them and smacked Erica's fiancé over the head with a log after the poor fool got out to check a "noise." Then the Count went up to the van, and there was poor Erica, knowing full well that something wasn't right. She made the mistake of looking out the van's little, tiny window. There was the Count, all fangs with a green, distorted face staring back at her through the window. Man, I almost jumped out of that chair, but not Dena Kay. There was no moving Miss Nerves of Steel. I would've left if my legs hadn't turned to Jell-O, not to mention I didn't know how to drive either.

So, of course, the Count's Long-Lost Love had to be bitten. The next day they acted like nothing had happened. On the screen, Erica started acting strange after her encounter with the Count. Her poor fiancé didn't have a clue. Then Erica got sicker; she needed some rest. BUT WAIT! Something wasn't quite right. Next thing you know, her friends see two holes in her neck and notice how Erica keeps trying to get away from them. Then they have to leave her ALONE, and just why I don't know. While she was unsupervised, Erica ate . . . GASP . . . a KITTEN! This was the last straw and just about killed me. I had violent nightmares and an upset stomach for days after that movie. Mother called it a "nervous stomach." All this didn't faze Dena Kay; she kept watching and shoveling down the popcorn during that whole darn blood-bath of a movie while I couldn't even look at my Whoppers after that.

If that stupid movie wasn't bad enough, we had a Peeping Tom in town and guess what . . . he liked to dress up as a VAMPIRE. I had overheard my mother talking to one of her friends about him.

"It's old Luther Collins," said Mother.

"Do tell!" gasped her friend Ava.

"Well, you know he's a little different, just a little on the feminine side," confided Mother.

"Oh no!" said Ava. "Who is he watching . . . men or women?"

"Well, I'm not sure about which ones he likes," said Mother as she frowned and gave Ava "that" certain look.

I was absolutely confused. Was Luther a real vampire or a pretend one? What did it matter if he was watching men or women? For heaven's sake, was he watching KIDS? Even more importantly, what would happen to him if he was out there peeping in somebody's window and ran into Count Yorga or that Cat Eating Woman? As if my vampire discoveries were not bad enough, my Cousin Tandy had informed me of a new threat to human kind: a bloodsucking goat called a Chupacabra. No wonder the coyotes howled at dusk. I knew there were all sorts of things hiding out there on Granddad's farm at night, and this new stuff just wasn't good. It was almost more than I could bear, imagining a demonic goat along with some crazy, redneck vampire running loose at night, playing dominoes down at the VFW club, eating chicken wings with his shirt off, and chewing Prince Albert while all the old men in town just thought he was a little "different." Somebody needed to do something. They needed to set old Luther straight or drive a stake through his heart. I wasn't sure what could be done about the bloodsucking goat. I sure didn't think Daddy would want to go out and catch it.

17 Ernesto and Hot Rods

Sometimes the music business got tough and gigs were hard to get, and so were part-time jobs for that matter. After all, the term "starving artist" applies to musicians, too. It was during one such slow time that Ernesto had to take odd jobs here and there so that he could eat. While he worked as a carhop at Scout's Drive-in Burger Joint flipping BIG BEANIE BURGERS, Ernesto dreamed. He swore that if he ever did make it big, he would get a super, hot-rod car. He really liked the cars in California. If there were people out there who really had fancy cars, it was definitely the people of the Ultra-Hip state.

Ernesto liked to dream about cruising Sunset Strip in a fired-up GTO or Corvette or on a Harley with a hot chick. He liked to look at those very cars while he walked about on the sidewalks. He didn't especially like driving his own car because it was an Impala in desperate need of shocks. When Ernesto approached a stop sign and hit the brakes, the Impala would bounce for several minutes after the stop. The same thing happened if he turned in quickly at Scout's. He didn't know that years from now, all this would be cool and people would actually pay to have their cars do that. Right now, all this bouncing made the tanned, sports-car-driving Californians just a little nervous.

Ever since he had that stoplight "incident," Ernesto was absolutely sure that Californians were crazy and mad, too. He had accidentally cut some guy off at the exit. He didn't mean to. It was just one of those occasions when you aren't exactly sure where you're going, and maybe you just decide you need to turn all of a sudden or you will get caught in some giant freeway loop that you can never get out of. Well, that's somewhat like it was that day when Ernesto decided that he suddenly needed to turn. So he did, and when he did so, he cut off some old man. This was even before the Road Rage Era had officially begun; this old guy was having a really bad day.

The Old Angry Guy followed Ernesto and exited when he did. Next thing you know, they were eye-to-eye at a stoplight. Then Old Guy said something, and Ernesto said, "Oh yeah?" Then they were both out of their cars. Ernesto didn't notice until he got out that Old Guy had something in his hand . . . and that something happened to be a machete. It was sharp, glistening in the sunlight.

"What the . . . HEY!" yelled Ernesto.

Old Guy didn't say a word, but swung. Ernesto jumped backwards. Old Guy kept silently swinging away . . .

"Hey man . . . what'dya doin'?" said Ernesto. "I mean, really, what'dya think YOU'RE DOIN'?"

Old Guy kept swinging, Ernesto kept running backward. *It's a good thing that I played football for the Fighting Steers*, Ernesto thought, *cause if I hadn't, I might not be able to run so fast backwards, and THAT coulda been a catastrophe.* Everything stopped. All those hurried Californians didn't budge. They sat and stared at the two guys: the hippie and a mean old guy with a blade.

It seemed forever, but finally Ernesto made it back to his car. Man was he glad to see that Impala. Old Guy got back into his, the light changed, traffic flowed, and life was good again.

☆ ☆ ☆

Ernesto even had another job at Hilo's Used Cars down off Hollywood Boulevard. During the day, he tried his hand at selling cars, and at night, he sometimes found his band a gig. The gigs were always in a cool part of town so Ernesto could still keep his ponytail and all that. Besides, this was California, and you just never knew when an agent or somebody important might walk in, even in a used car lot. Some people had been discovered waiting tables or working in grocery stores, like Marilyn Monroe or . . .

A guy Ernesto met in a coffee shop got him on at Hilo's. Ernesto pretended he didn't hear when Mr. Elmo, the owner had exclaimed to his friend, "Oh no, not

ANOTHER one . . . " But he landed the job anyway as one of the sales assistants had absconded with a battered Ford without paying for it. The police had to go and chase him down on the freeway, but it wasn't much of a chase since the car had already sprung a piston and began to sputter and die. The former sales assistant had no choice but to pull over.

Ernesto looked through the windows of the car dealership, but he didn't see cars. He saw success. He was just pure music, and he could be a popular musician like Steppenwolf, you know. The songs would just come, and this would inspire people to clamor to get his autograph. He could see it now—the audience screaming for more when he was trying to make his way off the stage. Girls would go crazy and throw undergarments at him.

Ernesto would have a vibrant, blue 409, and a babe . . . blonde, brunette, or red head, it didn't matter, with teased hair. He smiled about that. You see, he knew a girl back home with that big hair and long eyelashes who would look just perfect in a hot car.

"Ummm, EXCUSE ME. Do you work here?" asked a small man in an ugly suit.

"Uh, yes, sir, I do," he replied.

"Well, in that case, I would like to look at the Mercury Cougar you have out there on the lot. What model is it?" asked the man.

"Let's see here," said Ernesto, deflated from chasing dreams, back to selling cars . . .

☆ ☆ ☆

Ernesto had a cat named Simon. He liked to take Simon for drives in the California countryside and to the beach. Simon wasn't too crazy about the beach; Ernesto had put him on a leash and taken him out to play in the surf. Cats don't like the surf much, so when Ernesto saw all these neat little dog prints in the sand, he noticed Simon's prints—deep lines, all dug in, hanging on for life: two sets of claws, maybe all four. Simon was traumatized. They loaded him up, and Simon sulked as they headed south through agriculture country.

Driving down the road, Simon draped himself over the seat and stared over Ernesto's shoulder. Up ahead were fields full of cauliflowers and artichokes. Simon perked up; Ernesto had to slow down for construction. Next thing you know, Simon saw an opportunity for revenge and pounced out the window and out into the fields of produce. Ernesto pulled over and stopped.

"Simon, come on! Come on, Simon!" said Ernesto. He could see the artichoke plants parting like a small Red Sea up ahead as Simon skillfully maneuvered his way through the field.

Simon vanished into the artichoke maze. Ernesto started wading through produce, poking around plants. He looked over into another field and saw strawberries all around. You could just swoop down, pick one up, and pop it into your mouth. Ernesto then spotted a farm up ahead. "Simon, Simon, come on . . . "

Ernesto walked around looking for Simon for what seemed like hours, but to no avail. He turned and headed for the farmhouse. Ernesto clanked the door knocker, and a woman answered the door. She was slightly graying and heavy set.

"Hello, ma'am, I was driving down the road, and my cat jumped out and is running loose out here somewhere. By any chance, have you seen a gray tabby?"

"Uh, no," she said. "Your cat won't last long here. Coyotes, you know?"

"Oh no," said Ernesto. "But if . . . "

Then she shut the door. Ernesto felt his heart sink. If there was one thing he loved and needed all this distance away from his family, it was Simon.

From underneath the fern-like leaves, Simon blinked and wondered, *"What new land is this?"* He thought to himself how nice it is to be out of that car and away from the horrible wave crashing sounds. Too bad about the big guy, though. He had all the food, plus maybe he would miss him, just a little bit.

18 Art Comes to West Texas

The fourth grade brought color and culture to an otherwise harsh landscape. I decided to join a school group known as the Picture Memory Club. This organization had as its main purpose for all fourth graders, along with upperclassmen, to learn and memorize identities of the artists and the names of their masterpieces.These were European masterpieces, and they were painted by the masters of all time: Van Gogh, Cezanne, Renoir, Gaugin, Degas, Pisarro and the interesting paradox of Monet versus Manet. Such were the possibilities in culturally enriching extracurricular activities.

I was the ONLY fourth grader on the team. Eddie Logan and some others were also on the team. Of course,

I really respected his opinions, such as when he distinctly told me that even though I was a fourth grader, it didn't mean I would let the team down. I was determined not to mess this up because I knew Eddie was counting on me. Five students were on the team, and we practiced in the classroom. The only bad thing was that our practice time was during everyone else's recess. I guess there's a price to pay in becoming culturally literate.

Camilla Jones would sometimes give me a hard time, trying to trip me up in naming the artists, especially when my mind wandered—which it had a habit of doing at times. These instances occurred when I had had too much academic exercise and needed to get out and run in the sand, or loll around at the pond, or even kick back and watch TV. My thoughts would wander, and I would have to pull them all back and put them into my head again.

"What are you staring at out there?" Camilla demanded to know as I gazed through the windows.

It was a particularly sunny day without cold, heat, or wind—a rare thing indeed in this part of the woods.

"I'm just looking, that's all," I said.

"You're weird. You'd better concentrate so we don't lose the contest Saturday," Camilla said.

"Oh, Camilla, leave Billie Jo alone. She never lets us down," said Eddie Logan.

I turned and smiled, and Eddie stared out the window with me.

"What are you thinking?" he asked.

"Well, I was thinking that today might make a good picture in itself," I said.

"Why? It's just a day like all the others," said Eddie.

"No, it's not," I said. "It's just a little different. Look at the kids in the swings and how everyone looks right now, right there, just so." At that particular moment, it didn't even bother me that our school sat right on the edge of a wheat field, or that if you left your notebook out there alongside the grassy border you just might end up with a field mouse or grass snake in it. I mean, as it goes, we can't all live in Tuscany, can we? I thought it was partly being rural that kept people well rounded, honest, and willing to help others.

Eddie shook his head. He didn't see a thing different. He just didn't understand that somehow we were here for just this moment, and it would be over, and time would go on, and the old yellow bus would not come down Rural Route 38. He just didn't comprehend how much I loved this artwork we were studying and how a person could get lost in these paintings—when they were paying attention, of course.

☆   ☆   ☆

Maybe I was a little weird as I contemplated art and life when there were much bigger issues to deal with at school such as chalkboard races, forever regarded as necessary in the pursuit of mastering mathematics. I truly believe that such activity scarred me for the remainder of my life. I mean, after all, I absolutely hated math, not to mention when they threw in that whole x and y thing later on. I just couldn't see the necessity in it. I have always found mathematics to be a tricky science at best, and as for doing it quickly . . . that was outta the question.

Old Mrs. Carson, most pleasingly plump, her wide, black-framed glasses, pulled just so, would scan the classroom for math-resistant victims. *She was old*, I thought, because she had also been Beth Ann's teacher. Beth Ann was smart, and Mrs. Carson liked her a lot. I don't think she liked me at all because she was well aware of my inability to conquer mathematics. Mrs. Carson would stand there and stare at all of us, just so. Then she would slowly, painstakingly call out three names to go to the board. I always felt like something hit me in the stomach when she would invariably call on me. I would get out of my seat and walk to the board. With every step I took, the room grew in size, and the chalkboard seemed to move farther and farther beyond my reach. My feet were heavy and my head was hot. I could feel my face flush with the worst Flames of Affliction.

Mrs. Carson proceeded to call out problems: addition, subtraction, fractions, multiplication, and long division. Oh, the agony! EVERYONE was faster than me. I was, in fact, so SLOW I would lose track, and then I would have to sneak a glance at the person next to me. Sometimes it was nerdy Mike Adams, and I could hear the sound of his quick marks on the chalk—click, click, click, and presto change-o he had the answer. People would laugh at me, and Mrs. Carson would stare condescendingly through her glasses.

"Now, Billie Jo, redo it, and get the right answer," she would sternly say as my face became now a *thousand* Flames of Affliction. I prayed right there for lunch, or a fire drill, or for the marching band practicing outside to burst through the door, or for the office assistant to interrupt, or for high winds to blow off the roof, or for the Second Coming, or even a first coming, or for the fighting

Steers playing football to throw one long and hard right through the window and knock me unconscious!

☆   ☆   ☆

While I was quite miserable in math, physical education was a different story. When you are a girl and you grow up in the country and your granddaddy runs a farm, well, you are somewhat of a tomboy. Dodgeball was it for me— the highlight of a bona fide grammar school education. If you could master dodgeball, then you could master life. That was my philosophy.

"You are SUCH a boy," said Ruth Ann Howmet.

"No, I'm not," I said as I looked at her evenly. Sure, I had problems all right. After all, I was called Billie Jo just like that poor boy who jumped off the bridge in that song that involved some sordid mystery. That may or may not mean a darn thing.

"How do you catch all those hard hits the boys throw at you?" she asked.

Ruth Ann was mild and weak, but she was also quite good in math and knew how to generate those fast chalkboard clicks. My nanny says that a person can't do everything well.

"Everybody has something they can do better than everyone else," I said.

"You don't do dodgeball that well," Ruth Ann informed me.

"Well, I'm better than most the girls," I said.

She scoffed. I was ready for the game to start. The balls would come hard and fast, and you had to be quick. You had to jump like in *Kung Fu*, and you could trust nobody. Even the people on your side would sell you out.

I would hang around, successfully dodging the enemy until I was all that was left on my team.

Then some boy, like Freddy Hart, would throw a ball as hard as he could. After all, he was practicing to be a future Steer one day. Sometimes when one of those balls hits you, it can knock all the air out of you; sometimes it can pound your leg or sting your arm and heaven help someone if they almost caught it with their fingers, but didn't . . .

It was nice to be the only one left standing. It was nice to catch the final ball and to bask in the glow of success with the roar of the crowd in your ears when you just caught the hardest ball that Freddy Hart threw all week.

 **19 Lola**

Lola Lee Strickland was a small woman, probably not even five foot in height. She was the closest thing to an angel on earth I have ever encountered. She was tiny, humorous, and generous. So much so, in fact, that she once gave her last five dollars to a drifter during the Depression. He had come into the café where she washed dishes. Lola had taken this job when my grandfather found the one true love of his life, whose name was Edith, and then conveniently decided to run away with her, leaving behind my grandmother and six children.

The drifter who was down on his luck just happened to be passing through the tiny city of Rockville and had asked to wash dishes in return for a meal. My grandmother had told me that she overheard his plight and sympathized with him. She walked into the dining room and handed him the five dollars. Lola said to him, "I don't know where you're going, but hopefully this small amount will help you get there somehow."

My grandmother had known sorrow in her time, seeing death in many forms. She saw the demise of women in childbirth and had the opportunity of taking over three of her sister's orphaned children to raise because of that very occurrence. Life was hard in the country, even more so for the people who were not wealthy. She had seen men killed while working the land. She had heard the screams of the sick and the cries for the country doctor. She had nursed her own sisters, and before her life was over, she lived long enough to bury a child and some of her grandchildren.

One of the most vivid memories my grandmother talked about for years was the death of a young boy. Lola had gone to see friends on a Sunday afternoon with her sisters. The family they were visiting had young children. A little boy there had the face of a cherub with curly blond hair and chubby little hands. Somehow when the adults were inside and the older kids were playing, the little boy was playing around a wagon. He would peer through the spokes at the other kids and make them laugh.

When the women went out onto the porch to bring lemonade, the boy's mother looked up and saw the boy standing there. She told him to step away from the wheel, but he did not answer. A few moments went by, and they noticed he was in the same position, not moving. My grandmother recalled with sadness how the boy's head was caught in a wagon wheel and how he had choked to death without anyone realizing what was happening.

Lola's stories were varied: some happy, some sad, some all made up for me.

I liked lots of things about my grandmother, but I think I must have liked her hair the best. Lola had the most magnificent long, silky salt and pepper hair that flowed like disharmony. When she wore it all down, it went well past her knees. She would expertly twine it up into a tight little bun on the back of her head and pin it in place with those long, loose hairpins. Later, when she was older, it was a bit harder to position it in the back of her head, so she would sometimes braid it and wind in around on the sides. That reminded me of the future years of Princess Leia from *Star Wars*.

I loved spending time with my grandmother, especially when we had errands to run. She would grab her little blue pocketbook and don a head scarf and pull a sweater over her small shoulders. Then we would walk all over that little, dusty town, and I would look in every single store. Not that there were that many of them, but it was lovely to get out, especially after a nice dust storm.

☆ ☆ ☆

The M-System store stood on the corner next to the laundromat. It was not only a place to buy groceries, but a place to catch up on all the information you needed to know. It's how Grandmother and I both managed to stay so well informed. She always had a list, and everything had to be just exact because she wanted only the brands she liked.

"I'll need some crackers," she said. We walked along the aisle, and I grabbed a box. "Oh no, not those, Belinda."

"Which ones?" I asked.

"The Zesty ones," she said.

"I don't think they have them," I said, pointing to two vacant shelves.

"Well, I'll be," said Lola. "Belinda, see if you can find George." Mr. George was the manager of the M-System. He ran a tight ship, and he was always very helpful. I looked around. Up ahead, Doug Simpson turned into our aisle with a cart of boxes.

"Can I help you, Ms. Lola?" asked Doug. Doug spent a lot of time stocking the shelves at the M-System, and sometimes he would give all the kids one of those cheap, little round suckers if they had extras.

"Sorry, Ms. Lola, we aren't going to have those for awhile, but we have another brand here."

"Oh, no. That won't do! I can only eat THOSE. Why don't you have them?"

"Well, George had a falling out with the Cracker Man earlier this morning. I don't know what all happened, but the guy took what was here and wouldn't unload anymore."

"Oh, I'll be," said Grandmother. A world without Zesty crackers just never occurred to her.

"So the Zesty Cracker Man and George had a disagreement, and we can't get Zesty crackers here for how long?"

Doug shook his head. "I don't quite know, Ms. Lola. Hopefully, it will all blow over soon, or maybe the factory will make him come back here and deliver those crackers anyway. People gotta make money, you know. Anything else I can get for ya'll?"

"No, thank you. I'll just wait for those crackers. I can't eat the other ones," said Lola.

"Okay, Ms. Lola. Ya'll have a good day," said Doug.

One of the best places to walk by was the Osgood's Hardware Central Store. They had a marvelous fire truck in their window. It was long, red, sleek, and shiny, and it seemed to underscore the entire decade of the 1960s: loud, fast, wild, strong, bold. Something about that concept just fascinated me. It wasn't that I really wanted a truck, and the good Lord knows every female in West Texas needs a good truck, but this was colorful in a place otherwise devoid of color. I was simply mesmerized by it. In fact, it appealed to me almost as much as the plastic dolls down at the A&P.

My grandmother and I slowly walked into the grocery market. I knew that smell very well. The A&P carried the distinct odor of lunch meat, bread, and produce. It made me hungry. Lola didn't have time for me to loiter over the plastic toys because her dining chairs had to be recovered and the bathroom had to be painted pink. This had partly been Lacy Jean's decision. She was a color expert. Besides, I think bathrooms in California were probably painted pink. When Lacy Jean wasn't painting Grandmother's house pink, she was busy coloring her own hair a certain shade of blonde.

Down at the A&P, the old guys would sometimes gather, and every now and then I would get a free orange soda pop. I shut my eyes, felt the coolness of the bottle, and drank it down ever so gingerly. I had learned a long time ago that it did not pay to gulp an orange soda because you could easily trip up and have it go down the wrong way. I did this once under the gleeful, snickering eye of Dena Kay. It was so bad that the orange drink burned my throat, came out my nose, and even my eyes were crying orange tears.

"YOU. YOU. YOU!" laughed Dena Kay, "oughta see how red your face is!"

I decided Dena Kay should join the WAFS or the WAX or whoever they were and go make a difference in, say . . . Vietnam.

"Come quick, Binky," Grandmother called me by my nickname. I gazed at the plastic dolls. I noticed their painted blue eyes as the dolls stared wonderingly back at me. Troll dolls were at the end of the counter. They had hair the color of the rainbow and beyond. One troll doll looked exactly like the one Beth Ann had on her dresser at Nanny's house, the one that she had named "The Damn Thing."

"Now that's ugly," said Lola as she noted the vibrantly colored hair of the troll dolls. She turned up her nose and straightened her long, multi-plaid skirt. The patterns in Lola's clothes fascinated me. The plaids ran every way and then no way at all. "Come now, we've got to stop at the post office on the way home."

Only such a trip to the post office could launch me from toy gazing. The postal establishment was a red brick building. The front was glass with small aqua panels at the bottom. Since it was located adjacent to the tractor place, the workers would park big tractors and farming equipment right next to it. Despite the clutter involved in getting those life-saving nutrients from the earth, the tractor place could not compare to the post office. It was a highlight for me. I liked to go there at night when all was quiet, and you could walk in and stare at rows and rows of little boxes with combination locks on them and peruse the Most Wanted posters on the wall. Criminals and missing children stared back in unison, and I wondered where they all were. I thought about how and why people could just disappear and if they could ever be found.

I'd take my grandmother's hand after she had gathered her mail from P.O. Box 101. We would walk just one more block and arrive at her simple cottage house.

20 The Strickland Family

In the one hundred plus years of her life, nobody ever heard my grandmother say a cross word to anyone. ANYONE. She was the cement that held the maternal side of my family together. After she died, we all drifted away because the focal point was no longer there, and life as we once knew it was irretrievably lost.

Lola was supposedly of English descent and was also part of a family rumored to have Indian blood running wild somewhere among them. The Indian concept was strongly evident in the high cheekbones of both Sandy and Matilda Strickland—Lola's papa and mother—and even more evident in Matilda's quick temper. This was to solve another puzzle for me in uncovering my genealogical past. Try as I might, I have yet to find Indians at all in our part of Texas and not in our blood, either.

The Strickland Family came first to North Carolina from "somewhere over the water" and then finally came to Texas from Florida after the horror of the Civil War struck the deep South and sent many a man scrambling for a way to feed his family. Burton Ferrell Strickland and his wife, Mary Elizabeth Crawford Strickland along with three of their children, boarded a boat and sailed to the Texas coast. I wondered if they had caught that boat to escape the wildlife perils of Florida. This was because Mary Elizabeth had stepped on an alligator when she was young and almost lost a leg, not to mention her life.

She and her younger brother had been blackberry picking in a swamp in Florida. Mary Elizabeth just thought she was stepping over a log, but the log came to life. If it had not been for the persistence and quick-flowing adrenaline of Mary Elizabeth's younger brother, who beat the gator's snout with a long stick, I might not have been a young person lurking around the 1960s and then determining later what life meant and what my purpose for living exactly was.

My grandmother Lola told me a story about being abandoned in the woods by her mother. I found this appalling, quite frankly, as I was also a young child of approximately nine years old, and it reminded me of the story of Hansel and Gretel. Later, when I was older, I thought, *good grief, the woman had fourteen kids, maybe she wanted to pawn one or two off.* This was still not a really good excuse, even if you were like the Old Woman Who Lived in a Shoe.

When my grandmother was nearing one hundred years old, she suffered from what the doctor's called "Sundown Syndrome," and she would recall, in vivid detail, the quandary of a little girl left in the woods trying to find her way home. She wandered and called and nobody answered until a nice man in a buggy happened by, picked her up, and helped her find her home. She would call out, eyes wide with fear . . . "Benny, Benny, please take that little girl home." It must have been at that point of initial abandonment when Matilda decided that Lola's place as the least favorite daughter was doomed to a life of seconds and hard work.

Because of my great-grandmother Matilda's demands, Lola was housebound most of the time as a young woman. Matilda insisted that my grandmother go with her sister to Dallas when Maude had to have surgery. Even though my grandmother's family was comfortably upper middle class after her father struck oil on his farmland, my grandmother was given no money for the trip and had to sleep on the floor of her sister's hospital room as her sister doled out a small amount of money here and there for her to eat a little. It was just such treatment I thought about when I was older and my grandmother was telling me that she had absolutely no idea why she had lived so long. The obvious evidence to me was that Lola was a fine example of most lessons in the Bible that she so liked to quote, and my grandmother, like a few preachers I have known, had a light about her. The light sort of emanated through her and gave off that certain manner of saintly calm that comes only from inside a person. This quality is innate. You can just meet these people once and sense it and know it is there and that everything is all right.

☆ ☆ ☆

Miss Molly lived down the street from Lola on the north side. My grandmother was a good friend of hers. Lola used to take her a plate of food everyday because as Miss Molly became older she became confused. One Sunday morning, I went with Lola to take over the food. We walked up on Miss Molly's porch, and my grandmother knocked and waited patiently. We could hear Miss Molly shuffling inside. She opened the door in her pajamas.

"Hello, Molly," said Lola.

"Oh, hello there," said Molly.

"It's a beautiful morning, and we brought you some hotcakes and sausage."

Miss Molly's face lit up.

"So you can have your breakfast and get ready for church," said Lola.

"Oh," said Miss Molly, "I don't think I can go to church today."

"Goodness, Molly, why not?" asked Lola because Miss Molly never missed church.

"Oh, it's my roommate," said Molly. "She won't let me go; I don't think she trusts in the Lord."

Lola looked around, then down at me, and gave me a short smile. I could tell she was uncomfortable. We both knew Miss Molly lived by herself.

"Why don't we come in and sit with you while you eat your breakfast, Molly?" asked Grandmother.

"Well, I don't know. SHE doesn't like company," said Molly.

My grandmother was crestfallen. She took my hand. The rest of the afternoon, Lola could not read the *Three*

Little Kittens Who Lost Their Mittens to me for the 999th time. Instead, Grandmother had to go around town and ask folks about how to contact Miss Molly's son who lived in Dallas. She told me that it looked like Miss Molly would have to go to the HOME where she would have lots of company, be able to listen to piano music and church sermons, and even get a real roommate instead of a pretend one.

21 We've Got Spirit ... Yes, We Do!

"He's down to the 20, the 10, the ... TOUCHDOWN!" screamed the loud-mouthed sports announcer up in the little box at the very top of the stadium bleachers.

I yawn and try to see if anybody I know is running around down by the fence that frames the HOME side of the football field.

"Billie Jo, be still!" snapped Dena Kay.

"Shut up," I responded.

"Ewww, that's George Thacker," said Beth Ann. We all looked as Number 35 went running onto the field.

"Could Sarah Jacobs flip out any more?" asked Dena Kay.

"Oh, she's something all right," said Beth Ann.

She and Dena Kay surveyed the cheerleaders on the field: "Two Bits! Four Bits! Six Bits! A Dollar! All for the fighting Steers . . . Stand up and holler!!!!"

Personally, I thought the cheerleaders were okay. I was actually considering this as part of my upcoming teenage career.

However, the problem was the splits. My Cousin Tandy and I had practiced every day for weeks.

"We've gotta stretch more!" said Tandy.

"What? I already feel like Gumby!" I said.

"You have to work your leg muscles. If we keep goin', at some point, we'll be limber enough," said Tandy.

"At what point will that be? And will we be able to walk after that?" I quipped. We stretched for weeks and weeks and weeks. And still we could never get LIMBER or at least LIMBER ENOUGH.

"I think some people are born with a splits gene," I informed Tandy.

"No, that's not it at all," she said. "Maybe we could just be the cheerleaders for the Mustangs instead of the Steers. I don't think the Mustangs' cheerleaders do the splits."

I thought about changing teams since I was apparently going to be a failure at this process. "Maybe we will be more limber as we get older," I said.

"Umhmmm," said Tandy.

I sighed. I knew right then how tough it was to be a Southern woman. The prerequisites: be limber, have hair that you could either rat up or iron, not catch yourself on fire, bake doughy items, find more creative uses for Velveeta cheese, and learn how to handle various fowl.

I scrutinized the football field. Nothing seemed to be happening. Even Beth Ann and Dena Kay had ended their diatribe on the cheerleaders. *Oh Lord*, I thought, *football is boring, but at least they have chocolate bars in the concession stand.*

At the lower end of the field by the fence, I noticed poor Ricky Reinhart. Ricky was really old, about forty years old or something, and he was a little slow. He rode his bike all over town. He was the only child of an elderly, invalid woman.

I thought Ricky was nice and always shook hands with him. Mama Fern had said Ricky was "not right" and not to go around shaking hands with him. Dena Kay and Beth Ann didn't want to speak to Ricky at all and acted like he was invisible. Ricky had a football jacket that was emblazoned with ROCKFORD STEERS on the backside. He put that jacket on and rode his bike; sometimes he even wore it in the summer when the sun was beating down, the sidewalks were steaming, and West Texas seemed more like the Sahara Desert than part of the United States.

Even though Mama Fern and other folks said Ricky was not right, I found other people in town I thought fit in the "Not Right" category. Like Ernie Brewer. I had caught him trying to hurt my little dog, Cheetah. He was going to try to run over her in his fire-cracking car when I grabbed her from the street. He and his friends laughed and jeered at me, but everybody else thought they were okay because Ernie's father ran the insurance office and sold real estate.

Years after Ernie's tendencies toward animal cruelty had diminished, he had a heart attack on Main Street. My

Cousin Jerry was the paramedic on the scene, and Ernie grabbed his shirt. "Please don't let me die, please don't let me die!!!" he screamed.

Jerry didn't let him die that day. All I can say is it was a good thing I didn't turn out to be the paramedic on that particular day.

So to me, Ricky was much more right than anybody. The good-natured smile and those vacant eyes filled with merriment always made him a candidate for a friend. Ricky might forget who you were, and he would surely forget what the topic of conversation was, but he definitely knew right from wrong. In all the time I knew him, I never caught him trying to run over a thing on his bicycle: no small animals, no drunk pillars of the community, no nutty relatives, and no fighting Steers.

"Hey, it's fourth quarter!" Ricky announced from the fence line.

Mr. Adams patted him on the back. "I think we're gonna win this one, Rick!" he echoed.

"They gotta, gotta, gotta run the ball!" exclaimed Ricky, and then in the same breath he asked, "Who they playin'?"

"The Indians," said Mr. Adams.

"If they win this, does basketball season still start?" asked Ricky, hugging his purple jacket.

"No, we'll go to district," said Mr. Adams.

Down on the field, the final minutes were chalking up. The cheerleaders were jumping into overdrive, their teased heads bobbing up and down like Barbies gone wild. The game was TIED. Dena Kay and Beth Ann were in absolute concentration, meditation, and prayer for help from BEYOND. I was wondering exactly what was leftover in the concession stand and if it sold at a discount. I was also thinking about what Ernie's car would look like with a couple of flat tires.

"It's a snap, and it's INTERCEPTED by Number 22, and there he goes, FOLKS. DOWN TO THE 20, THE 10, THE 5, AND IT'S A TOUCHDOWN! The band broke out into the school song. The fanatical football fans went wild. And there it was . . . game over, but destined to be repeated many times in the State of Texas and even on this very football field. After all, it sums up Texas where a person's education is solidly built on a foundation of working at it and proficiency in passing the football.

Dena Kay and Beth Ann grabbed each other, quite pleased, of course. Earlier that day, the entire senior class had individually sworn that nobody knew a thing about how the word STEERS came to be solidly burned into the Indians' football field. I had a bad feeling about that one, a feeling that Retribution, like the Baptists, would soon find out, and I was really hoping my sisters were not involved in it.

I had asked my nanny why everybody had to be an athlete in school. She smiled. "Oh, it just seems that way, dear."

"I'm not any good at athletics," I said.

"Oh sure, you'll find something," said Nanny.

"Not like that."

"Well, anyway you're smart. That's what counts. You know what they say: we can't all be heroes. Somebody has to sit on the curb and clap as they go by," said Nanny.

22 Hardships and History

It was hard to believe that before I was a small child the Brazos River had been a powerful, thriving, gushing waterway. But it was. Back in the early days when the Germans and the Scots-Irish and the English settlers were taking on the daunting task of establishing West Texas, the Brazos was wild and flowing. The mud was red, the banks were tangled masses, and bobcats lurked in the trees. The Brazos was alive.

My grandmother Lola told me the story of a man who was trapped in that river with a team of horses. He didn't make it out. Two little children were picking wild blackberries and playing out by the river. They were supposedly members of the Jones family: little Sarah

Beth and Edgar Jones. As the kids were playing by the river, they heard shouts and looked upstream and saw a man with a team of horses in the water. Out there in the river, the horse team and rider were in trouble. The current was strong, and the horses lumbered to maintain some type of footing in it, but they stumbled on the slippery, jagged river rocks below. The wagon teetered. Then suddenly the horses and their rider were pulled full force into an even swifter current and from there were rapidly sucked out into deeper water.

"HELP ME!"

The children were at a loss; they were not big enough to find something to pull the man and a team of horses to shore. Sarah Beth wrung her hands.

Edgar bit his lower lip.

"HELP ME!" screamed the man.

"Run and get help, Edgar!" said Sarah Beth. It was the only thing she knew to do. So, Edgar ran back to the farmhouse to get his daddy, and Sarah stood on the riverbank and watched the man. The man with the deep-set eyes turned toward Sarah a third time. The man and the horses were now wild-eyed with fear. He held his outstretched hands to her. The wagon was coming apart from the beating on the rocks. Then rather quickly, the man and his two horses were pulled under for the last time, and the only thing left was the running river and the muddy rocks. Sarah Beth stared blankly at the spot where they vanished.

The farmers came out and searched the river for the man. Nobody knew of anyone missing, so the man in the river must not have been a local, but rather a traveler through the area. Little Sarah wondered about his family at home and how they would spend the rest of their lives thinking about what had happened to this man and wonder where he had gone.

I listened to the story of the man in the river with fascination, even though it was very sad. I thought of how he was there on the shore, trying to cross, thinking he could possibly make it over, but then the horror at realizing what was happening hit him. Every time we went driving along the Brazos River, I would look down at it, knowing that danger could rise quickly, even though it might look like only a mud hole in August. I remember thinking for sure if the river didn't get you, probably the rattlesnakes and cottonmouths would.

☆   ☆   ☆

Numerous pitiful stories of early pioneers exist. Needless to say, when you have Comanches flying down one side of Kiowa Peak and Apaches flying down the other, then you're in some pretty scary territory. These are two of the most warlike tribes that really didn't take kindly to the invasion of the white Europeans. Such was exactly the case in point at some time in the 1800s.

It was January in northwest Texas, and a bitter one at that. Sometimes it can be summer here in the dead of winter, but other times it can also be Arctic-like with snow and ice and a cold north wind brought on by a Blue Norther as those of us in this part of Texas call it.

A small group of English pioneers, the Pirkle family and a few friends, were trying to get set up here despite the uncommonly deep snowfall that year and the never-ending north wind. The problem, as my nanny told me this story, was the Apaches were not too happy about having these red-headed English people for neighbors, so they sent out a small party of warriors to solve this problem.

The Pirkles and their friends were caught unaware when the Indians came upon them there in the snow, and the justice that the Indians dispensed was swift and cruel. They took the two children and the mother and tied them to a tree. Then they bound the men and scalped them, but they were actually kind enough to kill them on the first effort. This swift end was not to be for the poor mother. The Indians scalped her, but she didn't die immediately.

The children were taken away to live with the Indians, but it was that poor Mrs. Pirkle who was left there, alone in that West Texas snow storm without her scalp, crawling through the snow screaming for help, for God, for an end to misery. In the end, some German settlers came upon her and found her frozen in the snow. The poor bloody woman was a testament to those souls brave enough to cross the water and settle the wild state of Texas.

Such sadness was even in my own family as my grandmother had recounted with great pain the burning of her niece and family. It seems that when winter actually came to West Texas in an extreme, it could always bring tragedy to those folks not accustomed to it. And it was cold during the month of February in this particular year, sometime in the 1900s—so cold that it killed lots of livestock and caused the ranchers great concern.

My grandmother's niece was the mother of four children; one was a newborn baby. They were huddling to get warm in their little, rundown farmhouse at the edge of the Strickland place, but the north wind blew relentlessly and the air seeped in. Bitter cold was all about. The cold forced her husband into action. He decided to extract some extra heat from the fireplace and poured kerosene into the flames. Well, that did it all right. The flames shot outward in an amazing arc blaze and set them all on fire. Some neighbors heard screams and saw the fire coming from one side of the house and ran in to get the family. They got them out and took them to the hospital in nearby Hashford, but they were too badly burned.

My grandmother's sister, the mother of the burned lady, was already at the hospital, helping tend to a sick friend when she heard that a family member suffering from horrible burns had been brought into the hospital. She had no idea it was her own daughter and grandchildren. That's the way it is sometimes—just like on a typical Wednesday afternoon when you're just living life in a normal fashion and something comes out of a blind spot and slaps you firmly on the right side of your face. Through the agony and suffering in the mid-1900s in rural West Texas where there was no technology or highly trained doctors, my grandmother's niece and family died as a result of their burns.

My grandmothers both told me stories of early days, not to make me suffer from chronic depression for the rest of my life, but rather to enlighten me about the people who lived there once, long ago, and to appreciate the life I had.

And that I did, right there in the mid-sixties like on a night that Tandy and I were spending together, and I did her hair all up with Dippity-do. It was all stiff, and I piled it high atop her head like a big ice cream cone, and we laughed under the covers. We both smelled really good the next day, just like Dippity-do.

23 Beth Ann

After Beth Ann graduated from high school, she ran off and got married. She married Raymond Evans, some guy who lived out of town whom she had met at a basketball game in another town, and my daddy sure didn't like him and neither did Nanny. I remember hearing Daddy yelling the day he got that news.

"That blank, blank, blank Hame-Headed-Hammer-Head . . . " I didn't have one ounce of an idea what a hammer head was, and this was way before the Discovery Channel and long before I knew about sharks with heads that looked like big hammers with teeth. I was betting that a Hame-Headed-Hammer-Head wasn't too good.

I really wasn't sure how I felt about Raymond. I did like, very much, to go with Beth Ann to visit him. It was a highway trip, and we would settle into the powder blue Ford and blast off with the radio blaring something about bad moons "coming up on the right" or was it "coming up in the night?" I could never exactly tell what it was they were singing.

After you got some miles behind you on the other side of Bingerville, like you were making a run for the Caprock, the country changed both in form and color. All of a sudden we were in a different land, a country with red hills and small canyons—the best part of it being the highway itself as it became a series of dips in the road. If I could talk Beth Ann into going fast when we hit the dips in the road, my stomach would do flips, and it felt for one brief minute like we were flying. It was marvelous to be in flight over the red hills and canyons and carved rocks of West Texas, sorta like rocketing along in a time machine, but without the Apaches.

Raymond was into cars, both literally and figuratively. He was kinda alone, as his mother was already well on the way to showing the signs of Alzheimer's. You either liked him, as he was loud-mouthed and bold, or you didn't. It was that simple. He was into anything that had a motor in it and used oil. Raymond had a best friend named Skip. They both spent hours under the hoods of cars, tweaking spark plugs, rebuilding carburetors, checking pistons, and changing rear ends. Raymond was a born mechanic, and he could talk to you about anything that had to do with cars. Owners of every car in that area of West Texas that didn't run right could seek Raymond out for therapy or new pistons.

Raymond's dream was to own a 409. I really didn't know what was special about this. Skip had one, but it possibly had everything to do with what was under the hood. You've never lived until you have witnessed a group of teenage boys dissecting an engine while the transistor radio played songs about wishing all the girls in the world could be conveniently located in California, all wearing swimsuits and knowing how to surf.

As the song played, I observed that Raymond did look quite a bit like one of the beach surfer boys in the picture in Beth Ann's room. That, I thought, must be the reason she liked him. I wondered if Raymond had ever tried to surf. I could almost picture him in a movie with Frankie and Annette. He was definitely a surfer guy; however, I wasn't sure you could do much surfing in the swirling sands of West Texas.

As I sat upon my perch, Beth Ann descended from the house with a large pitcher of sweet tea to revive the earnest mechanics sweltering in the Texas sun. Her hair and her skirt were both freshly ironed. She smiled at Raymond, and I really just didn't have a good feeling about that. I could picture them together in that little ratty car of his, a far cry from the dream, chrome-laden 409, his car without the floorboards in the back seat, and the shotgun sound that blasted whenever it was started. I could see the future: the three of us cruising into the sunset, and I dearly hoped they wouldn't make me ride in the backseat because I might fall through the holes.

Not too long after Beth Ann and Raymond got married, Beth Ann got pregnant: twins no less. I don't know, but once your sister turns into a young mother and doesn't get any sleep or have any money to buy pretty clothes, she sorta turns into a different person. Such was the case with Beth Ann; I kinda lost her after that. That meant that I had to make some new friends or become friendlier with the ones I had. I still had Tandy and that was good since we were the same age, and I didn't worry about her getting married in a week or a month or whatever. That would be on down the road.

Even though things were not quite the same with Beth Ann, I would spend some time with her and Raymond during the summers and observe their parenting skills from a distance. I liked visiting them during this free time as I pursued some of my hobbies and interests, plus Beth Ann got better TV channels where she was and had a small store that sold the best comics.

I loved the Archies; they were my favorite group of all time. They sang the "Honey Honey Sugar" song, and it sounded, well, rather sweet. Maybe that's why it was called bubblegum music; I always wondered about that. Tandy and I shared a mutual admiration for the Archies. In our world of copycat make believe, I usually had to be Betty because she was blonde, and Tandy usually was Veronica because she was brunette. I thought our Cousin Hank, the goddess, might make an excellent Mrs. Grundy.

The Archie comics supplied us with tons of insight into this world. We liked how they were always doing fun things, running around Riverdale in neat clothes and having a blast in high school. I adored Riverdale. Period. I could shut my eyes and picture that perfect little town; I'll even bet they had one of those big clocks on the square. What about that malt shop where they were always sipping a nice, frothy soda? I knew right then I didn't want to be a Steer or a Mustang; I wanted to go to Riverdale and become a teenager. But some confusion arose one day when Dena Kay so eagerly pointed out that all this existence was pure fantasy.

"You absolute, morons. The Archies are not REAL people," she announced.

I stopped chewing my Baby Ruth bar, ready for a fight. "Yes, they are. THEY are on the radio!" I said and looked at Tandy.

"No, they just had to get a group together when somebody came out with that song," said Dena Kay.

"They are real. They live in Riverdale, and they go to school there."

"Haaaaa!" said Dena Kay as she spewed Dr. Pepper all over the sand at my feet. "You two are SO gullible!"

"We are not gullible, whatever that means," said Tandy. And with that, Tandy grabbed my arm, and we marched off to the watering trough to discuss the matter with the cows and the goldfish.

I was a steadfast Archie's fan up until Donny Osmond came on the scene with the song "Puppy Love." I was sure he was singing "Puppy Love" just for me, and I was quite content to live forever thinking just that. Later on, after I grew up, I learned that it wasn't even Donny's song. It was actually some older guy, and he was singing about the Annette girl in all the beach movies, but it was all okay then because the whole Donny thing had worn off.

☆   ☆   ☆

When I was ten years old, my chief goal in life was to be
Cat Woman so I could cavort around with Batman and
Robin. I loved the way that gal could climb around on
buildings and jump all over the place. I liked her outfit,
shiny and black, and in my mind, I just knew what it
would feel like to rub my fingers over the leather or the
rubber, or whatever. I even liked the way Cat Woman
purred her threats. I would spend hours in the living
room of my sister's small trailer home constructing a city
in the corner and planning an escape route. I made my
own cape out of paisley print because that's all the spare
material she had, but I pretended it was shiny and black.
I practiced acrobatic feats—Cat Woman was definitely
for me.

Raymond had spent almost all their money on a car.
It was a convertible: a long, sweet Falcon convertible. If
you squinted your eyes just so, it could closely resemble
the Batmobile. I thought Cat Woman probably had a car
like this when she wasn't climbing tall buildings or being
a villainess: maybe on the weekends or something.

Sometimes, I would become weary of Cat Woman
while sitting in the large plaid chair in front of the TV. I
would glance up at the shelves Beth Ann had lined with
collectibles. I had a bank sitting up there. It was three
monkeys all sitting together on a limb: hear no evil, see
no evil, speak no evil, but at that time, I wasn't sure what
they meant sitting there like that. I had it chock full of
Canadian money some relative had sent to Nanny. I was
hoping to save up enough Canadian money to buy one of
those hoops with the attached ball that you put around one

ankle and jumped over with the other foot. I figured that was as good a way as any to increase my coordination, and I knew I would need to be very coordinated if I were going to take over Cat Woman's spot when she became too old.

About that time, I first tried dancing. This was really awkward since I learned all about dancing when I was spending some quality time with Beth Ann. Whenever I got tired of listening to newlywed spats and all, I'd attempt to determine the nearest escape.

One such spiritual journey for peace and quiet led me to Liam Jones. He lived in the apartment place. He was kinda tall for his age. He was standing under a tree when I noticed him, staring way up into the branches.

"What are you looking for?" I asked him.

"Oh, uh, it's my Frisbee. I threw it too high, and now it's caught in the tree."

"I see," I replied, staring up into the tree. "It's kinda far up there. Are you going after it?"

"Dunno," he said. "I may just wait for some wind to blow it down." He smiled at me.

I never really liked boys that much, but I did like his smile and the fact that he had dark hair—I was blonde.

"Hey, do you live here?" he asked.

"Oh no," I stammered, "My sister does. She just got married."

"Really? They live right there?" He pointed to it.

"Yes, they do," I said.

"Wow, I like that car," he said of the Falcon convertible.

"Yes, I do, too," I replied WHILE thinking of my current fantasy of driving it around as Cat Woman. *Ewww*, I thought to myself. I just wondered what Tandy would think about him.

24 The Bleak West Texas Landscape

Some parts of Texas you just have to live in to develop any fondness for. The one thing absent in West and Northwest Texas is trees, unless you count the mesquite. It's the most flat land anyone could dream up. Sometimes the mottled, brown landscape becomes its own desert. During drought, the corn, cotton, and wheat all scream at the sky wondering where God's grace is. I guess the earlier pioneers might have felt comfortable on this great, flat land because they could see the Indians coming for miles around.

I was always a tree hugger of sorts. It all started when I stayed at my grandmother's house. I would be outside playing in the hot sun. The sidewalks sweltered so you could even fry an egg on them. Inevitably, I would catch a glimpse of the mimosa trees that lined the front of her neighbor's house. These trees called to me with their long, silky, fern-like leaves and their cotton-candy-pink blooms. When they called, I went and played in the shade of their luscious environment. This was as close to tropical as you could get in the sticks. Under the trees, it was cooler and prettier, albeit for a short time, in the little corner of West Texas that exclusively belonged to my grandmother. Today, the mimosas are long gone. They have been replaced by some sort of bean trees that aren't nearly as pretty and offer no sanctuary to neighborhood children. The echoes still remain there. When I go outside and stare where they once were, I can hear them and even almost see them—the gentle limbs dangling their cotton-candy blooms in the sunlight.

☆　☆　☆

In the little town of right and not right people, there was Olee Olgither. Olee was a human machine, and he could get your attention fast. One day mother and I were passing through town when we heard a siren right behind us. My mother got really nervous.

"What is that?" she asked me.

"I don't know. An ambulance? A highway patrol?" I ventured.

This did not help matters any. Mother looked alarmed and quickly snatched at her cigarette to put it out.

"No, I don't see an ambulance. I don't even see a police car," she said.

I didn't see anyone either, and I didn't believe we had done anything wrong. I looked again. Then I saw him.

The red-headed Olee. He was chasing us on his bicycle and making a siren sound.

"Don't worry, Mother. It's only Olee Oligither."

"Who?" she asked incredulously.

"Olee Oligither."

"Who? What kind of name is that?"

"I don't know. Swedish or something."

"Oh dear, that poor boy can't think clearly. It's a shame." She clicked her tongue. "Somebody should do something."

I immediately wondered what could be done with him and why anybody would want something done with him; he wasn't a bad boy at all.

"You know, Olee doesn't hurt anybody," I said.

"Hmmph. No, only darn near gives people a heart attack," retorted my mother.

Mother wasn't having any of it. Chasing folks down the highway wasn't her idea of something that kids or anyone else should be doing. Traveling through Kahler or Hashford country wasn't always easy even when Olee wasn't on your tail. The infernal dust was always there, and learning to cope with dust is a definite must in Texas. My mother told me of a dust storm that hit the area in the fifties before I was born. In broad daylight, it looked like midnight. People couldn't see for miles and miles. The Baptists, Lutherans, and Methodists headed to the churches to pray in case it was indeed the end of the world. Instead of being the end of the world, it was just the end of farming for that season because the high winds had nearly ripped everything off their stalks. It looked like a big fan had been left on for a long time.

☆   ☆   ☆

Dena Kay and I would occasionally sneak in to swim at the old Traveler's Motel. There was a time when it was fresh painted and the pool was clean and had those little umbrella tables all around it. The desk clerk in the afternoon was chubby and usually asleep and never really cared about non-guests sneaking in to swim. I liked to pretend I was in Beverly Hills, and if I shut my eyes, I could picture palm trees just like on TV, maybe even like the ones on *Hawaii Five-O*. When I opened my eyes, I was far from Beverly Hills, and all I could see was one large century plant and the promise of an early dust storm from the south. In the evening, we could also come out here and look at the abandoned sewing factory that was opposite the motel. The entire west side was covered with large, black tarantulas. The whole building's walls were alive with furry black legs. I had never seen anything like it in my life, and I wondered where they had all come from and where they hopped off to during the daylight hours.

Dena Kay liked to keep me informed, and while we swam in the motel pool, she enlightened me regarding uses for the agave plant.

"They use them to make tequila," she announced.

"What's that?" I asked.

"Some type of alcohol."

"The stuff you put on bruises?"

"No, idiot, the stuff people drink."

"Well, that sounds just delicious," I said as I gazed at the prickly stems of the plant.

"You need to read more," said Dena Kay, sloshing water all over me with one big hand wave.

"You mean I need to read about grown-ups drinking alcohol? In that case I could just watch Uncle Roger every time he comes in drunk, falling all over the place. Is there anything we can do with the tarantulas? Maybe put them in a stew?"

She made a face at me and then dove to the center of the pool to touch the drain.

Thirty something years later, I pass by the old Travelers Motel. It's almost in ruins now, having long ago been vacated by folks brave enough to visit this part of the state. It looks lonely there. Weeds are popping up in the pavement and the pool is now all cemented in. The VACANCY sign dangles like lost hope. Even a couple of old, rusted, abandoned cars sit there. Either somebody forgot them, or somebody is gonna fix them up someday. The motel windows are boarded up, the little umbrella tables are long gone, and it is the most forlorn building in town. Looking at it now, I think it could be haunted by all those in the past who stopped there even for a little while to escape the ever-burning West Texas sun. Maybe they just needed to rest and have a cool cola in the respite of a swamp cooler and look out those little, flat windows. A whisper long gone: another symbol of a simpler time. The old hotels and diners are now empty. I wonder if I might finally end up here myself, inside the walls of the decaying motel. It would make a good ghost story after all.

25 Retribution

Mr. Alvo had a car with one of those little stuffed Chihuahua dogs with a bobbing head on the dashboard. Everybody thought he was Indian, but he spoke Spanish. He drove very slowly and favored one side of the road. The little dashboard dog's head turned half circles as its little, beady, black eyes surveyed the town.

My mother wasn't thrilled at all about Mr. Alvo; she didn't like him because she said he had a "shifty eye." Actually, he had one good eye and one lazy eye. This I noticed when he would stop and speak to us. He liked to talk to all of us Scots-Irish children in Spanish. This irritated my mother even more because by God, this was Texas, in the United States, where people speak English and people who choose to live here oughta learn the language.

"No te gusta tarea?" he would ask us about our homework with a chuckle.

"Do not talk to strangers!" Mother said to me.

"But there aren't any strangers here, Mother. We know everybody," I said noting the population sign of 1,929 strong.

"Listen to me," she hissed. "Don't talk to that old man. We really don't know much about him. He might not be nice. Got it?"

"Yes," I said weakly. I knew he would have to go over in the "not right" category, and I wondered if he and Ricky ever got together. I wasn't really sure if Mr. Alvo liked football. I was really curious about him, and I wanted so desperately to ask him how he got that name. I thought that maybe I could get my Cousin Jesse to ask him. It was worth a try, and perhaps I would be rewarded with some wild west story just waiting to surface under Mr. Alvo's sun-wrinkled skin.

Jimmy Earl was my other cousin who was Jesse's age. They constantly hung around together, sorta like bad news or dirty laundry. I decided to hunt them down to see what they knew about Mr. Alvo since they were older and wiser and that oughta be good for something.

I found them over by the Osgood's store on their bikes. They were drinking colas, laughing out loud, and snorting Dr. Pepper through their noses.

"What are you two up to?" I asked. They looked at me as if I were the Scourge of the Earth.

"What's it to you? Why are you here?" they demanded.

Apparently, I must have interrupted something important. "Ya'll haven't been throwing any grass snakes at girls have you?" I asked.

"Nah, we've moved on from that," said Jimmy Earl.

"Oh yeah?" I said.

"All right, what'dya want? Hurry and get out of here because we are busy," said Jesse.

"Hank has a new boyfriend," I announced smugly. He scowled at me.

"So what? She's gone anyway," he said. I smiled. I had no idea how many boyfriends Hank had had, but it was good to get to Jesse. "We have more important things to do now."

"Like what?" I asked.

"We're going to play basketball at the courts," said Jesse.

"Yeah, we're going to see how many balls we can bounce off somebody's head, like the dunce boy," said Jimmy Earl.

"Who you calling that awful name?" I demanded.

"Aw, it's just ol' Danny Wells," said Jesse.

"That's not funny," I replied.

"Sure it is," said Jimmy Earl. "It's pretty darn funny."

I shook my head. I was glad I wasn't a boy. They were not smart, and not only that, they were just plain mean. I didn't even want to ask them about Mr. Alvo after that. I just turned around and headed back to Grandma's house because it was Wednesday, and it was also Gingerbread Day. I could at least hope that poor Danny didn't make it to the basketball courts with those two idiots on the loose.

☆　☆　☆

That night I had a dream. I was way back there in the Wild
West somewhere. Indians were with the white Scots-Irish
settlers, and they didn't get along. I think I was actually
the large oak tree situated there in the Indian camp. A
tree with many eyes. Mr. Alvo turned into Geronimo in
my dream. He was apparently the Indian chief's brother
or something. Mr. Alvo-Geronimo was sitting on the left
side of the chief, and he had a feather in his headband.
He scanned the teepees with his one good eye and his one
lazy eye. Then two warriors appeared. They had Jimmy
Earl and Jesse as hostages. Jimmy Earl's and Jesse's eyes
were wide with fear and dread.

"Tie 'em up," said the chief.

"Then burn 'em," said Mr. Alvo-Geronimo.

"But . . . but . . . but . . . Wuh . . . Wuh . . . Wuh, we're
friendly. Wuh . . . Wuh, we're just plain friendly white
people," stuttered Jesse.

Then Hank appeared. She must have been an Indian
princess or something. She had a headband and Hawaiian
flowers in her hair. She had ditched her mermaid fin.

Jesse saw Hank and was immediately struck dumb
with overpowering love. But it was not to be. Jesse had a
date with Destiny. He and Jimmy Earl had been caught
torturing a poor, mentally impaired Indian boy, and that
was an unforgivable sin. There was a lesson to be learned
here.

Then I saw Ricky riding his bicycle through the
teepees and cheering for the fighting Steers, and Mr.
Alvo-Geronimo turned slowly to the chief with mischief
shining in his lazy eye. He and the chief shook hands,
and the chief turned to the warriors.

"It's time," the chief said slowly.

The warriors bent down in unison to light the fire, and then I woke up. The sun was shining. The birds were singing. All seemed fine. Apparently, Jesse's and Jimmy Earl's lives were spared because they were still with us, plotting their next escapade.

26 Coffee Anyone?

Cecil White was the cook at the Korner Café on the highway. Sometimes he could cook up the best chicken fried steak and gravy that could ever be served in the South—when he was in the right mood.

Cecil hated the coffee drinkers who came into the café everyday. After all, all they did was drink coffee with the same cup, refill after refill for hours on end. The coffee drinkers didn't make a dime for the restaurant. Sometimes when the coffee crowd really wanted to splurge, they would add a honey bun to their order. These honey buns had to be heated because why in the world would a person want to eat a cold one? Cecil had to heat them in the large, dilapidated oven that closely resembled the fiery furnace of hell the Baptists sang about on Sundays.

My mother liked Cecil because he was something of a local hero. He had managed to foil a burglary attempt on the restaurant when it was in the process of being broken into—he was on his way to work. He ran over to the gas station, broke a window to get to the phone, and managed to save the $20 or so in the café's cash register. Therefore, it was okay if I talked to Cecil. Sometimes I liked to talk to him because I thought I would probably have to learn how to cook something someday. Besides, he gave me free food.

One day old Verna Parks came in to drink coffee. She fascinated me because I liked the way she painted her lips. I don't think she had lips at all, just a series of lines that framed her mouth. She wore bright red lipstick that ran into those lines of wrinkles, creating red stripes all around her mouth. At the end of the day, the lipstick might very well end up all over her face, seeping into those creases and spilling outward. Sorta like Baby Jane, as I was to discover later.

Verna decided she wanted a honey bun, and she must have it warmed in the oven. So the waitress took the sweet roll in to Cecil who opened the big, black monstrosity and proceeded to warm it in the furnace of LIFE OR DEATH.

The waitress delivered it to Verna who promptly remarked, "Not hot enough," and sent it back. She did this again when the waitress brought it back. "Still not hot enough. I like 'em burnt."

Cecil hated the haul back into the kitchen. It was hot in there. The big, black oven was hard to operate; it loomed in the distance, like a slightly disabled dragon. Cecil pulled open the heavy oven door and put the honey bun in the oven. He left it there, and left it there, and left it there. When Cecil finally retrieved it and sent it out to Madame Verna again, it looked like a piece of charcoal.

Verna hated to admit defeat, so she gracefully accepted the honey bun but managed to leave it on her plate untouched as she had to retouch her red-lined lips and rush off to attend her paper route.

27 Dodging a Smoker

My mother tied her headscarf around her hair securely and jumped into the big-nosed Buick. At least, that's what she always said about Buicks. She was on her way to Kopper City to check on a sick friend. As she pulled out of the driveway, she noticed that the Broom Man was out again. I could only imagine what she said to herself.

Mother had been wary of him ever since he attacked the neighbor's son late one night when he came home from a date. "I thought he was gonna jump through my windshield," said Greg.

"Really? What happened?" asked Mother.

"Nothing. Nothing there and then the next minute he pops up out of nowhere, whacking my windshield with his broom. I thought I had run over him!" said Greg.

"My, oh my!" said Mother, clicking her tongue.

She looked wearily down Maple Street, and sure thing, the Broom Man was out today, sweeping the streets. Sometimes he chased people who walked their dogs because they got too close to his yard. I think he liked a really clean yard and a clean street. I was careful to walk on the other side. He never bothered me any, and I always liked his boots. Mother was just a cautious woman who sometimes got headaches and had to lie down. She drove by slowly, keeping her head turned straight; however, she did check the rear mirror when she saw Broom Man muttering to himself.

Past Maple Street, Mother then headed south on 287 and had just the luck to be stuck behind BIG AL'S BBQ truck that was toting a smoker. Smokers are legendary in the Land of Barbeque; every Texan knows that for sure. She made a mental note that it might just be time for some nice ribs again.

Big Al took his barbeque seriously, too. He believed the secret was not just in the sauce, but how the meat was cured and smoked thoroughly for hours on his wonderful, black-painted smoking machine. He was proud of that machine and hauled it around to the many events that were held here. These festivities included the Watermelon Festival, the Churned Cheese Festival, the Cotton Crawl, the Wheat Flogging Parade, Chicken Day, and Makin' Kahler County Proud Day.

You could take a bite of Big Al's barbecue and just be in heaven. And he barbecued everything: chickens, brisket, steaks, hot dogs, sausages—you name it. He used to laugh and his giant belly would shake like Jell-O. He'd say he was fixin' to go make a meat run, so I guess he just loved his job.

But that particular day, my mother wasn't in the mood for barbeque. She was considering changing her hair color maybe to red or a light brunette, or something, and she was contemplating this life-altering event those remaining few miles to visit her friend.

As luck would have it, the smokin' machine somehow managed to become detached from Fat Al's truck. It started wobbling at first, then swaying from left to right, and finally, much to my mother's horror, the smoker came loose from the truck and plowed into the front of that big-nosed Buick.

I wondered, as Mother relayed the event to us, if all those sausages, smoked quail, and hams were launched into the air. A veritable feast, I thought, and quite a good meal for the coyotes.

Fortunately, Mother had at least slowed down, and she wasn't hurt at all when the smoker struck. In fact, every dark curl was still in place and not a smudge on her Max Factor lipstick. The car damage was bad, and she was mad because she was also late to her see her friend. Mother had to postpone that trip due to lack of transportation. I was glad Olee didn't show up, sounding his siren and all, making Mother even more nervous. I figured Olee must've been watching *Popeye* or chasing the peacocks on that particular day. I would have also hated to be Big Al, too. Because, unlike most of us other Nordic-influenced folks in this area of West Texas, my mother didn't take after the Scots-Irish in that she seemed to be descended from another sort of dark European race: people with flaming tempers and little tolerance.

28 Coyotes

I loved to spend the night with Nanny and Granddad on the farm out in the middle of flat nowhere. It wasn't as bad as you may think; there was lots to do and lots to wonder about. It was especially fun when Tandy and I got to spend the night together in order to ponder the universe.

One thing that always did scare me at night were the coyotes. Of course, everybody knows these small wolves are more afraid of humans than the other way around, but when I was young, I was not so sure of that. They would come out at night and start howling, and Tandy and I would sit by the screen door and listen to them. It was almost like living in Transylvania, for we both truly believed they were bloodthirsty animals that would emerge from the darkness and spring on us like werewolves, rip us to pieces, and drink our blood. Sometimes Tandy and I would get a flashlight and sit under the covers and shiver as we listened to the coyotes sing their nightly haunting songs.

"Why do they do that every night?" asked Tandy.

"I guess they're hungry."

"Oh . . . Do you think their eyes are red or yellow?"

"Don't know and I hope I don't get to find out! I'm glad the chicken pen is sturdy."

"Yep. Why don't we go watch Johnny Carson with your daddy?"

"Good idea." Then we would get up and tiptoe to the T.V. room where Daddy was usually snoring through Johnny's monologue even though it was funny and all that. Sometimes if he wasn't snoring, we would find him laughing at Johnny's humor. The television would invariably wipe out the sound of the bloodthirsty coyotes, and we could forget about them for a while. Then maybe later we would move on to other unexplained phenomena like the Phantom, Bloody Mary, and light switches.

☆　☆　☆

Other mysteries existed out on that farm. Tandy and I were concerned about a lunatic who supposedly roamed the countryside at random. The only problem was, we never knew of the lunatic actually doing anything to anybody. Or for that matter, we never knew of ANYONE ELSE actually seeing the lunatic. But, of course, we all knew he was there, waiting to sneak up on God-fearing people and do whatever injustice a lunatic might do in the West Texas desert.

On days that Tandy and I had discussions about him, we were afraid he might be stalking us from a distance. Of course, he'd better not be out in the wilderness at night because of the coyotes and all. Nevertheless, we would look for his shadow behind an old outhouse my grandparents had before plumbing. We never actually saw anybody, and the truth is probably nobody would have been able to find Granddad's farm unless they knew it was there. That is just how far out in the middle of nowhere we were.

On the No-Lunatic-Is-Stalking-Us days, we enjoyed the plain sunshine and swings and not much to worry about. Tandy and I sat under my grandmother's grape arbor with its big leaves and juicy purple fruit. We watched the big-eyed cows chew slowly, dreamily, from side to side. We swam with goldfish in the too-small pond and made mud pies until we couldn't stand it anymore. We walked to the mailbox on the rural route and walked back. We rode my sister's bicycle down the long, winding, tree-lined driveway and picked blackberries until we were sick at our stomachs. These were the lazy days of summer heat that were incredibly long at that time, but somehow have invariably become much shorter since then—even shorter for those unlucky souls who couldn't escape the coyotes.

29 Crime in West Texas

It was perplexing to me that in all the peace and quiet of Kahler County there was a definite criminal element present. This fact presented itself to the fine citizens when the local barbershop was held up. The problem was that the barbershop was located right across the street from the police station, a fact my mother loved to ridicule. This was the topic of conversation one particular afternoon when my mother and grandma were sitting at the kitchen table shelling peas.

"Can you believe it?" Mother asked. Right across the street. Now you tell me that they can solve anything here when they can't find their butt with both hands???"

"Hmm . . . " said my grandma, shaking her head. Lola was never one to criticize anyone, especially law enforcement officials.

"I think that is even worse than the time the gas station was held up by that crazy woman with the water gun," said Mother.

"Was it really a water gun?" asked my grandma.

"Oh, yes," said my mother with a smirk on her face. "And she got all the way to that roadside park almost to Saymer."

"How much money did she get?"

"She got $13.85, and that was on a good day. Probably that old sheriff Rusty Hawkins was in charge of running down a crazy female criminal, and he couldn't find his butt with both hands either!" mocked Mother.

I thought it odd that people needed both hands to do something that stupid. But it was Friday, and I was entertaining myself yet again, setting up a big box in the corner of my grandmother's living room where I was busy hard at work as a store clerk with a shoe box for my cash register. I was a bit irritated at my mother because she would not give me real money, so I had to take Grandmother's writing tablet and make my own money. It was hard drawing George Washington on all the bills I needed.

"Did she escape from the institution?" asked Grandmother.

"I believe she did. I think she used to have a cot set up downtown in Abilene where she would sit and put on makeup and stare at the traffic. She must've stolen that car. It's a wonder she could drive. Nobody had any idea as to where that poor, sick woman was headed . . .

probably she didn't even know herself. Not a one of those officers are worth a darn."

"Well, how about that Mike fellow? He seems pretty nice."

"No, he's an idiot, too. He told me that when things look too rough to handle, they go and put their Wrangler jeans on so they won't tear up their uniforms if they have to get down and fight." Mother broke into laughter. "Could you see any of our crew actually fighting to take somebody in?"

Grandmother clicked her tongue and tapped her finger to her chin. A sure sign of serious thought processes.

"You know, take that messed up Luther Robbins. One day they said he was wanting to harm his wife."

"Oh dear," said Grandmother.

"Well, you know they had the car chase after him in his pickup truck and all that. They ended up making him crash in the alley next to Pearlene's Beauty Shop. And wouldn't you know it, all the officers were over on the driver's side, thinking they were gonna fish poor Luther out that way, but while they were occupied trying to get in there, he'd already escaped out the passenger side and was three-quarters the way down Main Street before they ever figured out he wasn't even in the truck!" said Mother.

"I'll be. What happened to him?"

"Oh, they gave him a ticket and locked him up for a few days to cool off."

I wanted to ask if Fat Al had gotten a ticket the day of the smoker accident, but I thought better of it and rang up a sale of $13.85 on my register.

"You know they really ought to do something about that Peeping Tom," ventured my grandmother.

"Hmmph, they'll never be able to catch that weirdo. I heard the other day that Norma Jean Brouchette poured some hot water and chicken gizzards on him."

"Really?" asked Grandma, her eyes widening while pondering the concept of the necessity of chicken gizzards. "Was it boiling, you think?"

"I don't know, but she is from Louisiana, probably the swamp—maybe she had a little voodoo mixed up in that."

I caught a glimpse of my grandmother's face. She was looking truly worried over these past events in our local community. I wondered myself how we would all manage to be safe in this town full of robberies, Peeping Toms, and traffic violations. I thought for sure if one could get through this, then why worry about growing up and going to a big city. I decided to watch a new adventure of *Buffy and Jody* on TV and leave the town happenings to Mother, who seemed to handle it very well. Buffy and Jody had an attractive life there in New York with the park right out in front of the penthouse and all. The only thing that disturbed me was how high up they lived. Personally, I was quite afraid of heights. I sure hoped Buffy and Jody would never fall out one of those windows or off the balcony.

30 Sea Monkeys

Something about the back of magazines always appealed to me. They were just full of advertisements for all sorts of stuff in the comic books and the teen magazines that my sisters read. It was simply amazing what a person could order from the back of the magazine. Jesse had told me about some X-ray glasses he wanted; they allowed you to see right through people. I surely didn't think he needed those; he had to have been up to something bad. My magazines didn't have that, but one day, I found something that I thought was absolutely glorious—INSTANT pets.

Yes, indeed, there, right in front of me, in fine black and white print, was an ad for Sea Monkeys. According to the text, these creatures were wonderful miniature little primates. You could order a package of some sort and then put them into a fishbowl and—Voilà—you had new pets and for only seventy-five cents! What a deal! I just had to have some because they looked so darling. The more I examined the ad with a boy and a girl about my age gazing into the fishbowl obviously astounded at the little Sea Monkeys dancing, turning flips, and waving to the children, the more I knew I needed them.

So I decided to first approach Dena Kay. I should've known better because Dena was never interested in donating money to any of my causes, including my need for pets, companionship, and various toys.

"Look here, Dena Kay, aren't they cute?" I asked.

"Go away," she said as she twirled her Maybelline mascara.

"It's not much money," I continued.

"No, freak," she said.

"I could do something for you."

"Go ask someone who cares."

I sighed. "Are you gonna wear lipstick, too?" I had to ask as I thought about Verna's lips.

"Get outta here now, will ya?"

"ShareEEE, ShareEEE, BabEE . . . " blared from the radio.

"You can play with them, too."

Dena Kay looked at me with one clump of mascara frozen on the right eye. "Moron, you can't play with them; you can't take them out of the water. You can only sit and watch them. Besides THEY ARE NOT EVEN REAL."

Well, that's what she said about the Archies, and we all knew better than that.

"I wanna dance, dance, dance . . . right on the SOMETHING, SOMETHING when the beat is really hot," screamed those surfing dudes from the radio.

"Are you going to the dance?" I asked Dena.

"Get lost brat!" she yelled as she finally noticed the clump of mascara.

Such episodic attempts at bonding with my sister were exactly why I needed pets. This was because I was quite simply alone and had to make my own fun. It would take years to evolve into one of these morbid teenagers. I ended up having to get the money from my mother. She actually gave it to me although she wouldn't budge on the red fire engine I also wanted.

"Because you ARE a girl! Freak," smirked Dena Kay.

A girl or a freak? Which one? I wanted to ask, but let it drop.

So I went with the Sea Monkeys. I filled out the order form myself and took it off to the post office. I just couldn't believe that I would have to wait six long weeks for the Sea Monkeys to be shipped from somewhere in New York. I felt for sure it wouldn't take a truck six weeks to drive from there to here. I resolutely decided to wait it out as I deposited my mail on the inside drop in the post office where I happened to run into Lacy Jean, my favorite cousin.

"Hi, pumpkin," she cooed at me.

It was flat amazing how different Lacy Jean was from Dena Kay.

"Hello, Lacy Jean. Whatcha doin'?" I asked.

"Oh, I'm just filling out my paperwork to compete for the next Watermelon Queen title."

"Really? That's so neat."

"Yeah, I'd really like to do it. I think it would be lots of fun."

I kinda liked the idea, too—a real-life queen in our own family. I was wondering how we would get all that mile-high blond hair stuffed down into the tiara. If she won, maybe I could get some special privileges just by knowing her.

"What does the Watermelon Queen do?" I asked Lacy Jean.

"Well, you have to have your picture made when you are all dressed up. You have to go around to other towns to tell them about the nutritional value of watermelons, smile a lot, and tell everybody how good watermelons are, and all that sorta stuff."

"Wow," I said. I thought she would be absolutely perfect for the job. I could just see her posing for pictures and waving to the crowds. There would surely be a lot of boys there eating watermelons. That was a given. I even liked watermelons, too; it was almost my favorite food next to my grandma's chocolate pie. I counted up how many queens this county could possibly have as I mentally tapped them off: the Cotton Queen, the Christmas Queen, the Queen of the County, the Peach Queen, and I thought I was probably missing a few of them. Lots of queens here for sure . . .

"Watcha mailing today?" asked Lacy Jean, pulling me from queen enumeration.

"Oh, just my order for some Sea Monkeys."

"What's that?"

"Oh, they are some new kind of pets."

"Hmmm, sounds like fun," Lacy Jean gushed.

"Yeah, I think it will be."

She smiled. "Come have ice cream with me later, pumpkin."

"I sure will and lots of luck with the watermelon people. I really think you are the one."

"You're too sweet," said Lacy as she patted me on the head.

I stood back for a moment and had to admire Lacy Jean. She was the epitome of what a small-town woman in Texas just oughta be. My own image, staring back at me in the reflection of the P.O. boxes, was nothing in comparison. There I stood with one thin wisp of fine blonde hair hanging in my eyes and wearing clothes that by the end of the day could use a pretty good scrubbing. I also had two scratched knees at the time because I had to maneuver to the top of my grandmother's shed to retrieve Mrs. Dudson's cat who was not cooperating with her at the moment. No, Lacy Jean was special all right, and she should definitely be the next Watermelon Queen.

I left the post office with my mail order dreams, and after what seemed an eternity, the Sea Monkeys finally arrived. I was so excited after having been depressed for leaving the backroom window open and freezing my hamster to death. I got the fish bowl water ready just like the instructions said. Then the magic moment came when I opened the freeze-dried packet of Sea Monkeys and poured them into the water. They looked exactly like tiny specks of dirt, but they were definitely moving around in the water. I do have to admit they were a little small, and I couldn't really see them waving their hands and turning flips like they were doing in the magazines.

"I can't see them," said Dena Kay.

"Sure you can," I said. "They're right here. Just see how they're swimming around and doing tricks?"

"Those are just dirt specks in some water. You need glasses," smirked Dena Kay as she pranced off to her room for round two with the Maybelline.

I pouted and tapped the side of the fish bowl with my finger. I was really hoping that the monkeys would grow some so I wouldn't have to pretend that I actually saw them doing things. The next day I awoke and all those tiny little black specks had settled neatly on the bottom of the fish bowl, and my instant pets had apparently gone into early retirement.

31 Mama Fern

My mama was as strong a woman as there probably could ever be. After all, making a life in this inhospitable section of Texas isn't the easiest thing around. Now, unlike the rest of us bona fide Scots-Irish, mother obviously took after her father's side of the family. For one thing, she was short and dark, where my father's side of the family was tall and blonde. Mama Fern also lacked that certain sense of humor and the mischievous nature that made those neat little crinkles turn up at the corner of my father's eyes. She was, in fact, a rather serious woman with quite a temper when she was "riled up." My mother had the ability to beat the heck out of her throw rugs and to transfer that skill for use on people, if the need ever arose.

Now I was the youngest of three girls so I believe maybe she had mellowed out some when it came to me. There were times when I did act up, and my mother would grab me firmly by the arm and tell me that I had better straighten up and fly right. Every now and then I did know what it felt like to have her hand swat me firmly on the bottom. Most of the time, however, I was quite successful in escaping my mother's wrath and having it turn around on my sisters: one benefit of being the baby of the family.

My mother grew up in Hashford County primarily on the Strickland family farm where she had loved running through the cornfield with plants that reached high to the sky, at least whenever there wasn't a drought on. She grew up rough and fast with her own two brothers and two half-sisters. My mama was probably even more of a tomboy than I was since she never backed down from doing just about anything that the boys did.

My mother and my aunt Donna both were fine examples of West Texas women. They could bake, clean, hoe the weeds out of the grass, iron, do laundry, and even throw back a shot of whiskey if the occasion called for it. Housework was something that was taken seriously and had to be done, no matter what. My mother could simply not keep enough Lysol or Clorox bleach in the house. The Clorox bleach was by far her favorite tool as she instructed me:

"Clorox bleach will kill EVER kind of germ there is."

I nodded my head and agreed that it was definitely a good thing to know about bleach.

☆ ☆ ☆

One of my best memories is of a lunchtime when a nice skillet of okra was frying on the stove and a big roast was in the oven along with mashed potatoes, black-eyed peas, and an apple pie. This type of food later became known as "comfort food," but let me tell you, at that particular time in the Sixties, it was also pretty darn comforting. During one such time, Aunt Donna and Mother were bustling about the house while Miss Lynn Something Or The Other blared on the radio musing about the current state of life in Topeka, Kansas.

"Right here in Topeka, . . . falling rain, dripping faucets, and the bawling, babbling kids," she sang.

I thought that probably summed up just about everywhere in Texas, too. The whole darn state was full of leaky faucets, bawling kids, babbling babies, and frying okra. Still, it was good to know what was going on in some of the other states, too.

I think there were two Miss Lynns. That one was not simply the queen of country music in West Texas. Oh no, she was even more than that. She had a status that I firmly believed approached sainthood, and that's pretty darn good in the Bible Belt. The women pronounced her name as LOWRhettTah, and I think the pain she sang about in her songs pretty well reflected the majority of women in the South: the drunk husband who stayed out all night, the lack of new clothes to wear, the endless chore of raising children, and the flat pure message of being under appreciated. I think my mother, Aunt Donna, and all their friends knew exactly where she was coming from.

☆   ☆   ☆

The one time I observed my mother's full-blown temper in action was when we had temporarily relocated farther out in West Texas so she could help take care of her cousin Edna who had been diagnosed with cancer. Of course, my family was not well known in those parts, and neither was my mother's penchant for complete cleanliness. That is what almost did Edna's neighbors in.

It so happened that Cousin Edna lived next door to some people who also hung their clothes out on a line right next to hers. One day we had a big wind that was nothing out of the ordinary because, in my opinion, the farther west you travel in Texas, the stronger the darn wind will blow. Well anyway, as luck would have it, between the wind and whatever, the neighbors were "missing" some clothes.

I had not a clue as to what was up when I was out playing by the clothes line and one of the children came out to taunt me about "white trash that stole other people's clothes." I had no idea what she was ranting about, especially since my mother was a fashionable size 6 and hers was a barbeque-appreciating size 24. So I went inside where Mama Fern was making up a fresh batch of baked apples and relayed this new information to her.

"Oh, they said I'm white trash and I steal other people's laundry, now did they?" she asked.

"Yes, they did," I said.

"Well," she said as she dried her hands off on the dish towel. "I'm stepping out for just a minute. I'll be right back. You just sit here and watch these apples cook."

Now my mama was small, but she was also loud and could get to the point very quickly. She went next door and paid the neighbors a visit, and I really think she got the whole "White-Trash-Stealing-Laundry" episode straightened out quite nicely because those people never did mention it again.

While she was there, I would also wager that she gave them a good sermon on cleanliness and the countless reasons not to wear somebody else's clothes or sleep on someone's linens that you don't know and maybe a free opinion on Clorox bleach. Anyway, after that happened, our stay with Edna was quite uneventful, and the neighbors next door simply tiptoed around my mother for the remainder of our visit.

 32 The Baptists

They simply don't call this part of the country the Bible Belt for nothing. As far back as I can remember, from the 1960s forward, the Baptists have been a vital part in keeping God here in West Texas where he oughta be. There are usually more churches than anything else in most of the small Texas towns, and folks really do have a wide choice. There are the Pentecostals, the Methodists, the Church of Christ, the Catholics, the Believers, and maybe a few lesser-known groups that maintain the status quo.

People in small Texas towns need salvation, and these are the folks that make sure we are gonna get it. If anybody new moves to town, they are at the doorstep the next day asking them about such things as where their church home will be, do they know their Savior, and if they have any idea what will happen to them when they die. These folks like to get right to the point.

I always liked the Baptist Church because the preacher there had a sense of humor. He used to put a saying out on the billboard every week. One of my favorites always came around in August when the sign read:

"And you *think* it's hot here . . . "

The Baptists were also really good about getting people to actually feel what would happen to them if they didn't change their wicked ways. Every Sunday as I sat next to Grandmother, the preacher would invariably finish with a shouting stance regarding fire, brimstone, and eternal pain. I always thought with that particular consequence, it was a good thing that we had a church on every corner. My mother had a neighbor, Mrs. Beasel, who was an extremely devout Baptist. She even traveled around to other towns where she listened to people speaking in tongues and watched them receive on-site healing from some gifted man of the Lord. Mrs. Beasel was a complete comfort to the community as she always made the rounds when somebody died, toting a congealed salad, casserole, or chocolate cake. I particularly enjoyed chatting with Mrs. Beasel because I liked seeing her wearing vibrant colors to compliment her orange hair. You see, Mrs. Beasel didn't have the talent for at-home coloring techniques like Lacy Jean had, so she got different results. I thought that was just fine because her heart was in the right place, and her cooking was really delicious.

☆ ☆ ☆

Only one time do I remember when shame cast a shadow over our religious community. That particular event brought about a period of amnesia where people quite simply seemed to forget about it. It involved a streaking preacher. Now this all happened a bit before the seventies when people starting running around athletic events and political functions nude on purpose—even before mooning became a popular sport. This preacher was such a nice man nobody could tell from the outside that he had these inward impulses to be naked in public and lounge around roadside parks.

My mother thought it was hysterical, as she would, of course, think in that manner. My grandmother thought it was horrendous and would simply click her tongue in her mouth. I had a hard time deciding what to think as nobody would talk about it in front of me, and I had to sneak around to eavesdrop when the adults were discussing HIM, which I did one day as I found Mother, Grandmother, and Mother's friend Lula having coffee.

"And they found him out at the roadside park, naked as a jay bird," hooted my mother.

"You don't say," said Grandmother.

"How do all these perverts find us?" said Lula.

"Oh, I'll bet he came out of Abilene, too," said Mother.

"Didn't he have a wife and children?" asked Lula.

"Yes," said Grandmother.

"I don't think his wife really cared anything about his hobby," smirked my mother.

"That's right. Didn't she turn funny on him?" asked Lula.

"He definitely turned pervert on her," said Mother.

"Well, where all did he go around here naked?" asked Lula.

"Oh, they saw a naked man around Hashford, and Rockville, and Kahler City, and actually I think there were several sightings," said Mother.

My grandmother looked duly mortified. "And to think, a man of God . . . " she said.

"Maybe he just felt inspired by nature," laughed Lula.

"Well, they got him out of town pretty fast, too," said Mother.

"Now we won't have a preacher for a while," said Lula. "It's hard to get folks to come out here."

"Yes, it is. It's hard to attract people to this paradise," laughed Mother.

"You know that poor Mr. Woods? I think he's a Pentecost," said Lulu.

"Oh, yes. I think someone had to finally come and get him a few days ago," said Mother.

"Really?" asked Lula. "What was he up to this time?" she asked.

"Oh, he was back to trying to make diamonds out of peanut butter again. I think he almost blew up his carport with whatever he was mixin' that peanut butter with," said Mother.

"Methane gas?" asked Lula.

My grandmother clicked her tongue in her mouth. Spiritual sorrows and idiocy were heavy burdens to bear.

While I sympathized with the bleak state of our doomed spirituality, I still had to figure out how to fight boredom on my own terms. Since the demise of my Sea Monkeys, I was back to entertaining myself, or as my grandmother called it: "making my own fun." I thought I would just walk down the block and take a look at the new church they were putting up. The building had a sign out front that boldly self-proclaimed it as a "Spiritual Powerhouse," and it all sounded pretty good to me. After all, any sort of a powerhouse coming in among the mesquite trees and the tumbleweeds would certainly be good for the community.

33 Traveling Farther West

Cousin Edna was one of the lucky ones, as she was actually able to beat her cancer, make a recovery, and move out by herself in the country. So, of course, we took a little vacation that summer when school was out to spend some time in far West Texas located on the outskirts of the Pecos River. I didn't know Miss Edna well, as she was my mother's cousin which made her my something-something-once removed. I looked forward to meeting her, and I did like the trip over the bridge getting to her house as it was narrow and quite a long ways down.

From way above, I could determine that the rocks were both pretty and sharp. It was just a bit disturbing how the rocks sorta cut out through the water even though some of them were quite lovely with their red and gray colors. There were some old bridges people didn't drive over anymore that Dena Kay and I had found on one of our expeditions. Of course, she dared me to walk out into the middle of one, but I was too afraid, noting the long drop between the canyons. I decided in one of my past lives I surely must have been pushed off a mountain top.

Now I wasn't all enthusiastic about this trip. First of all, I was stuck with Dena Kay since Beth Ann was all married and starting a blissful, new life. I couldn't take my Cousin Tandy with me, and I also hated the prospect of not staying on my grandparents' farm because I much preferred that type of summer vacation. I simply lived through the end of school in order to arrive at this point that consisted of three months of pure bliss, although bliss was bound to be hot and dry. Nanny told me everything would be fine, and it was always good to try out other places for a while. So I gathered my stuff and climbed into the car with Mama Fern and Dena Kay, and we were off to discover what new adventures lay outside of the Law West of the Pecos.

This part of Texas is quite important because it was around Pecos where Judge Roy Bean sometimes held court in a small saloon. He was well known for dispensing justice with pure Texas flavor. Apparently, he was quite a character as he was in love with some British actress and wrote her many letters. It was said that he asked her to visit this wild part of Texas and also to take a tour of the Chihuahua Desert while she was at it. I would imagine, if I put myself in Miss Langtry's shoes, that offer was probably really hard to refuse. I would like to have seen her face when she thought about going to hang out with some drunk, chubby judge who was as well known for swindling as he was for justice keeping. I could only imagine how Miss Langtry would fit into some godforsaken area of far West Texas with the heat, the bobcats, and a bunch of cowboys with missing teeth. The funny thing was, however, that Miss Langtry did finally take him up on his invitation to visit, but she came too late. The illustrious judge had managed to drink himself to death before meeting his true love.

During this vacation, I actually managed to expand my Spanish vocabulary because a large part of the population was Hispanic. Sometimes they were not too friendly to small but tall, Scots-Irish girls who were all too nosy. I somehow managed to find a few friends close to my age who taught me some essential phrases so I could feel more at home.

The best person I met all summer was a girl my age named Mandy. She loved horses, and she had several of the Arabian kind. Actually, horses were pretty big here, even bigger than where I had come from. Mandy was great. Her family had been one of the original pioneer groups that settled this part of Texas, and they had been in the ranching business a long time. She told me stories about the area and about attending the little school there. Mandy said some of the teachers were very mean, and I knew how bad that was as my first-grade teacher had slapped me on the back with a ruler for not coloring within the lines.

Mandy said that her teacher for the past year was a man whose name was Mr. Youngmun. He was German or something, and he had a strong temper. Mr. Youngmun especially took fault with kids who used the word "yeah" when they were called upon. It was of utmost importance to always answer "Yes, sir" when addressing him. If you were busted for using "yeah" in the classroom, you had to go up in front of the class and stand there. Mr. Youngmun admonished students publicly in front of their peers. Mandy said this very thing had happened to her one day and caused her to hate the fourth grade and probably diminished her educational experience forever. I certainly identified with that as I personally felt that mathematics had completely ruined my life.

Visiting Cousin Edna for the summer really didn't turn out half bad because Mandy had more than one bike, and she had loaned me a red and white one with a banana seat and those long v-shaped handle bars. I was so busy with Mandy and her friends that I didn't even have time to torture Dena Kay, except for knocking her radio off the trunk of the car during an Archies' song and making a wide-open run for it as she chased me with a coat hanger. She then lost her footing and ended up kissing the gravel driveway. After that, Dena Kay accused me of ruining her knee for eternity. She was certain she would be a cripple, and I would have to live with the guilt. Turns out, down the road, I would end up seeing a movie that discussed in great depth the principles of coat-hanger discipline.

☆   ☆   ☆

Mandy taught me a game that the older kids liked to play. She invited some other kids over that day, and we played spin the bottle. Now I really had no idea about this, but Mandy thought it was hilarious. We sat out beside a little storage house in her back yard. Mandy had invited Freddy and his brother Allen and their friends Rubin and Valentina. We took a coke bottle and set it in the middle.

"Now what do we do?" I asked Mandy.

"Just take the bottle and give it a good spin," she said. "Whoever it lands on, you have to lean over and give them a kiss."

"What?" I asked incredulously.

"It's no big deal. It's just for fun," said Valentina. I spun the bottle first and it landed on me. I was quite happy. Then everyone else had to spin it, and they all ended up kissing each other.

My final spin landed on Freddy. I could feel my face turn into a fiery pit. It was as if we were all sitting there, frozen in time at the edge of the desert with the soft neighing sounds of the horses in the background amidst the sharp clucking of the chickens. It was almost like I could get up and walk away, and they would all remain there spinning that coke bottle on and on and on.

"Come on!" screamed Mandy.

"Don't be a chicken!" said Valentina.

So I leaned over and kissed Freddy, briefly on his lips, and he stared back at me with dark eyes that bespoke of complete disinterest. There it was, and the whole THING was over in a second.

"See, it's no big deal," said Mandy.

Too late. I had already decided that spin the bottle was not a game that I really wanted to play, at least not for a very long time.

☆ ☆ ☆

Mandy taught me how to ride horses, although I had already had some experience with it. I also never liked riding all that much either, but since she did, I went along with it.

One day we were in the little town outside Pecos, riding along through the large, dry drainage canals when we heard the sound of music. "It must be a party," said Mandy. "The locals here have parties all the time."

"Oh, yeah," I said.

As we approached the next street, the music became louder, and I listened to the Spanish lyrics to see if I could make out any of it. We saw a group of kids running barefoot and chasing a hog.

"What are they doing?" I asked.

"Darn, it looks like they're having a hog killing. They have a name for that, too, but I can't remember what it is," said Mandy.

"Oh, gosh," I said. I was never one for livestock slaughter, despite being a Texan and having to dodge that same thing on my granddad's farm. After all, I did have that nervous stomach and a deep-seated fear of heights.

The hog was running everywhere. Then my horse jerked his head, and I saw the hog again as it ran almost out in front of us. I could see that it was bleeding, and the wild children were chasing it down the narrow streets. The horses jerked wildly. This also made me nervous. I was duly appalled at having to witness the celebration of the pig and hoped to never see such another spectacle for my entire life.

"Why do they stab it here and there and chase it around?" I asked.

"I really don't know. Some type of custom they have," said Mandy.

The hog whined and screamed, and the kids ran, and the whole landscape, the cacti, the trees, the brown grass, melded together around me. I wanted to go home then and there. I was dismayed at this type of hog killing; even my granddad was more humane than that when he killed them, which I knew he did. He always tried to do it when I was away, or he would send me into the house and tell me to stay. I had watched him once, he and a group of men. They had taken the hog and hung it upside down from a tree. Then they made the cut, nice and clean across the throat. I had sneaked to the window to watch and saw the whole thing through my nanny's white lace curtains.

The last I saw of the hog, the kids were still chasing it. The drunken adults had taken a few more stabs at it, and the hog had finally become so weak from blood loss that it succumbed to the mob. I don't know what went on after that as they were boiling pots of water in the yard, and the women were bustling in and out of the house. The music played loudly, and there were distasteful smells emanating from the house. I turned the horse back and went on my way to Cousin Edna's house where I was going to demand that my mother get us out of this slaughterhouse the very next day.

34 Ernesto Gets Close

Ernesto was devastated over the loss of Simon. He had asked his friend Joe to go back to the fields with him and look for the cat.

"I think we should play Simon's favorite song," said Joe.

"You think it'll work?" asked Ernesto.

"Why not? He's a music cat. Likes the Beatles better than the Stones, likes early Yardbirds. It's all good. Let's do it."

They jumped into the car and drove out to the fields. Dusk would soon be upon the countryside. Ernesto turned up the radio and "Whooo are you . . . ?" blasted out of the speakers.

"You think it's too loud?" he asked.

"Na, man. It's all good."

"Let's get out and see. We have to be careful. The lady in that house doesn't like me much." So they took off walking through the fields. Up ahead they heard the sound of horses neighing.

"I could get used to this," said Joe. "These artichokes are like . . . CRAZY."

Then Ernesto heard something. "Was that a meow?"

"Whoo are you . . . ?"

They rounded the corner, and there he was: one extra-tired, not-so-smug cat.

"Simon!" exclaimed Ernesto. Simon was glad to see him. Ernesto scooped him up. Simon's eyes slightly divulged his fear. Had he learned a lesson?

"Yep, that cat. He's a music cat, all right," said Joe.

Simon was happy—even happier to climb back into the Impala, but now with windows closed.

Looking around the fields flung out before him, Ernesto remembered home—the coyotes first, the armadillos second. "Do you think there are armadillos around here?" he asked Joe.

"Oh, man, I don't know. That sounds more like a Texas thing," he said.

"Yeah, you're right," said Ernesto. He remembered a time when he had run away from home and hitchhiked, trying to get back to Viney. He had boarded a bus and gotten off in West Texas, heading out on foot. First, he saw one armadillo on the highway. Then another, and another, and then more. It was almost like a sea of dead armadillos on the road, like a bad dream. He was practically having to walk on the road stripe, while keeping an eye over his shoulder for cars. Dead armadillos. Everywhere.

"Man, what was it? Armadillo mating season?" he asked out loud.

"What???" said Joe.

☆ ☆ ☆

Back into the LA party scene, Ernesto planned his future and the future of his band as major players in the world of rock 'n' roll. One day while he was cruising the beach along Santa Monica, he met up with a music agent, Mr. Jeffrey Clark. This guy seemed to be on top of things, and they decided to have a drink in a pub to discuss the many routes that would best serve Ernesto and his band and get them before the right people.

"There's a gig coming up in lower Belmont called Santoria," said Mr. Clark. "I would like to hear your band, and if you guys are any good, maybe we can do something."

"Sure, I can get everybody together, and we can try it out," said Ernesto.

"You do have some original stuff, right?" said Mr. Clark.

"Oh, yeah. I think we've got a definite sound."

"Well, good. Here's my address. I have a setup in my garage, so give me a call when you can get everyone together."

"Sure thing, and thanks a lot, man." He couldn't wait to tell the guys that they finally had a chance to play for someone who could possibly help them. He was tired of Mattress Mania, and he just flat refused restaurant work. Man, why did it have to be so hard? All this show business stuff, plus the fact they weren't that good looking. What was the world expecting? The Dave Clark Five?

Ernesto hurried back to LA to the Crestview Apartments where he would be before the other guys got in from their jobs. He climbed the two flights of stairs up to the apartment they were all sharing. It was crowded, and it was a rotten complex. He was going to put his key in the door when he noticed it was ajar. He went in. The place was ransacked!

"No!"said Ernesto. But he already knew. Their instruments were gone: the drum set, the keyboard, the bass guitar, everything of value taken out of the two-bit apartment. He sank into the middle of the room with his head in his hands. There would be no way to play now because they didn't have the money to buy more equipment. It was a chance, a shot, and the meddlesome hand of fate had pointed a black finger at the band from Texas that might have been and that the world would never know.

Ernesto called Mr. Clark to let him know they couldn't play, but he decided to go to Santoria anyway, just to see who was there and what kinda sounds would be coming down. He caught a bus and went to the concert. The medley of bands was pretty good. Some were more talented than he knew the Dirty Ratfinks were, but he liked the music mix. Just as he had imagined, there were lots of women there—lots of pretty ones in the front. How lucky could you get—if you had a band, that is.

It was getting late. Ernesto was debating whether to stay for the end when the announcer screamed:

"Okay everybody. Let's get ready for the band of the hour, the one, the only . . . . . . SanTanAh!"

Ernesto could hear his heart beating when they took the stage, and the guitar strung out the opening for "Black Magic Woman." Ernesto had a plan. Maybe he could slip around back and talk to them. Why not? It wouldn't hurt. Just to meet the band. What a happening thing. He made his way through the crowd and as close to the front as possible. Just as he had suspected, there were police officers at the stage openings. He had no way to distract them. He thought of saying he was Santana's cousin, but surely that had been tried before. He walked closer and the officer moved in front of the entrance. The officers gave him an empty, level stare. He had no choice but to turn around and call it a night.

35 Pa Buck

My mother's father was called Pa Buck, or "daddy" as the girls simply called him. I really never considered him my grandfather since he had taken off when the children were still quite small. So as my grandmother had no use for him, I found out that I didn't either. It was interesting when he came around back though, mainly because of one outstanding fact: he had a monkey.

The monkey's name was Albert, and he usually traveled in a cage in the back of Buck's pickup truck. He wasn't a nice monkey at all because his formative years had mainly been shaped by teasing cowboys who gave him drinks and chewing tobacco. Therefore, I was not allowed to play with the monkey. I had strict orders from my mother. She just knew he would bite me, and I would get God-knows-what-kind-of-disease and end up being a Rabid Maniac Girl with a nervous stomach for the rest of my life.

My Cousin Jerry and I used to hang out by Buck's truck and talk to the monkey. I refused to let Jerry tease him because I felt sorry for him. I really wished that they would give him to me, and I could take him out to Granddad's farm. He could straighten him out, and then the monkey would be happy. He would learn to like the farm. I wondered, however, how Nanny would react to having a monkey out rounding up the livestock and feeding the chickens and the goldfish. *He might even help her put up her fruits and jelly*, I thought. After all, monkeys were supposed to be very smart. Try as I might, I could not persuade Buck or Uncle Roger to let me take him.

☆ ☆ ☆

The Greenwood family was English as far back as anyone could trace them. They originated in the Yorkshire area of England, an area that was hard hit by Viking raids during early English history. This seems to play out in the appearances of some of the early family members who were described as tall, having blond or sandy hair, blue eyes, and most likely big feet. Back in the 1800s, if you were six foot or over, you were classified as a giant, so the description was quite probably true.

Buck's grandfather was a man named Japheth Greenwood. He was a blacksmith during the Mexican-American war and had been stationed around San Antonio, Texas. That's where Japheth caught the measles, became horribly sick, and had to sit out of the conflict for some time. This might have been a stroke of luck because if he had been able to continue on, he might have found himself at the Alamo, and we all know how that turned out. For his service in the army, Japheth received a land grant in Eastland County Texas.

Now Eastland County is another place in Texas that is almost as darn near hard to farm as it is in Kahler or Hashford County. But for several years, Japheth managed to tough it out as he was descended from a rough line. His father, John, fought in the Indian raids in Arkansas, and his mother, a large Scottish woman, had nine children and did farm work as well as any stout farm hand along with housework and cooking—the typical pioneer life.

Japheth's uncle had described John Greenwood as a "scoundrel, a ne'er do well." What that exactly meant, the family descendants were never able to figure out, but needless to say, family members didn't get on well with John. When Japheth was about sixty years old, he submitted papers for a pension. In the documents, Japheth described his physical limitations. He also stated that he had some "droughty land in a droughty county." This phrase should probably be adopted by the Department of Agriculture as Texas descriptive terminology. I think he nailed Texas farming right on the head with that assessment.

36 Where Have all the Good Cowboys Gone?

When you grow up in Texas and then go other places, everybody thinks that you automatically have horses to ride, oil wells in your backyard, and a Cadillac with horns on the hood. That simply isn't the case, although owning an oil well or two wouldn't necessarily be a bad thing in my book as it has done wonders for some people.

Texas is synonymous with cowboys; you just can't escape the lure of the legend. It's not a bad stereotype at that, but even when I was little, there seemed to be very few real cowboys lumbering about and even then, hardly any men walking around in hats. Nevertheless, a working ranch is a working ranch, and that's the closest thing that

I could ever discover when I was little and wondering about cowboys.

We also had rattlesnake cowboys whose job it was to go out and catch the snakes and put them in toe sacks. This was during the Annual Rattlesnake Festival. I could only imagine all those sacks filled with teeming, squirming, not-hardly-happy snakes. What if you had a bag where at least two of the snakes didn't like each other? Once they were caught, the rattlesnake cowboys would have a show at the school where they put all the snakes in a glass aquarium type thing so people could come gawk. I can't say anything here because I liked to gawk, too. Sometimes the snakes were huge; sometimes they were curled up; sometimes they tried to strike. After looking at the snakes, one could really work up an appetite for barbeque and watermelon. I'm not sure what happened to the snakes after the show, but most likely somebody got new shoes or a belt or something because surely they didn't take them back and let them out.

Pa Buck and Uncle Ted used to go out riding horses. They weren't looking for rattlesnakes either. They just had stuff to do. They wore the cowboy uniform: hats and Levi jeans. I have a photo of one of their daily jaunts when they took the horses out on Uncle Ted's land where they rode out between the mesquite trees and up around the catfish tank where I learned to fish. I remember watching the graceful prance of the horses as they waltzed over the ragged, parched country, their silky manes blowing in a light breeze. I would sometimes climb up on a tree limb to watch Pa Buck and Uncle Ted until they became tiny dots in the distance, their plaid shirts a blur of mixed color.

Despite the aura of cowboying implying something special, sometimes it can be a dangerous thing. This lesson I learned as a little girl when my Uncle Ted was almost killed when he was roping a calf. As Uncle Ted threw the rope, the horse stumbled and fell, and it happened in such a way that the horn of the saddle went into Uncle Ted's head. I remember my mother getting me up early and driving to Abilene to see him in the hospital. He was in intensive care because he had to have brain surgery. Nobody thought he would live.

It seemed that we went to the hospital for weeks. I wasn't old enough to go up to the room, so Dena Kay and I would have to wander around downstairs. We spent so much time there I became quite familiar with the floor plan. I would see the green and gray colors of the hospital at night in my sleep. Sometimes we would just sit in the chairs and stare out the windows and look at the city of Abilene in the distance, all around us.

"Dena Kay, have you ever been in the hospital?"

"Nope, just when I was born."

"I don't think I would like being here."

"Well . . . Gee, you won't have to."

"Oh, I don't mean now, but someday you know. I think older people have to spend a lot of time in the hospital."

"Yeah maybe, but some older people just spend all their time in the rest home."

"I think the pictures they have up here are creepy, too."

"Yeah, it gets very tiring in this place," she said as she contemplated her new silver and blue eye shadow kit.

"And there isn't even anything good on TV." I glanced over to the black and white television in the corner of the snack bar. I had eaten everything in those machines, several times, and I was missing my grandma's hot rolls.

"Yep," I said. "I sure hope we don't ever have to stay in a hospital."

In the years to come, I would also think of my Cousin Hank in the same cowboy spirit. She had some bad luck in her family when she was a teenager. First, her mother died of cancer, then her oldest sister, Connie, was diagnosed with it, too. While Connie was in the hospital, her other sister, Janie went to see her. As cruel fate would have it, Janie was killed in an auto accident on the way to the hospital to see her sister. So after Hank's oldest sister Connie died, Hank was left an orphan without siblings. Since the family was gone, the only solution was for Hank to go and live with relatives, an option she didn't wish to consider in her bitter grief.

Hank donned her black leather jacket and grabbed a small bag and climbed on the back of a Harley motorcycle with some guy she had just met. She got on that motorcycle and rode out of Arizona to parts unknown, and we never saw her again after that. When Hank struck out for her future, I, too, was woefully sad. I wondered what would ever happen to her. Would she become a drifter or decide to head off to Mexico or live in another foreign country somewhere?

In my dreams, I envisioned Hank with her long red hair flowing behind her as she stepped up onto the back of that Harley and wrapped her arms around a leather-clad figure. Then they both vanished against the burning amber of an Arizona sunset. A few years later, I would recall her many times. I could see Hank as though she were standing right before me. I would think of her and wish that I could have just a little bit of the fire that seemed to emanate through her and weave magnificently through her long, red hair that framed those fierce eyes of green ice.

37 Tornados

There is one good house in town that has a lot of windows and sits on a hill. The realtor who sold it last time pointed out quite adeptly that the view was panoramic, and she was right. The best thing about the hill house was that at this place a person could see which way the tornadoes were coming.

It's an absolute curse that this part of Texas has to lie flat dab in tornado alley. Even the fake ones are scary. My mother can attest to this as she recalled one day when she was outside hanging out clothes and saw a dark funnel cloud overhead. She pitched the clothes basket down and yelled at my grandma to get in the car, so they could pick up Beth Ann from school. The thing was, it wasn't a real tornado that day; it was a plume of smoke from something being burned.

Sometime in the 50s, a bad tornado had struck Knoxford City. It wiped out a large portion of the town, including heavy damage to the hospital. So for quite a time after that, people took dark things in the sky rather seriously.

Spring is an interesting time in Texas: the days can start out warm, and then a Blue Norther can hit and drop the temperature like a bag of bricks thrown into a lake. The time before storms actually hit has always mesmerized me. The clouds start rolling in, and depending on what time of day it is, the sky sometimes turns pink. Maybe the rain will hit first, at times coming down with a vengeance, and then many times hail will follow closely and make the most horrendous pounding noise on the roof.

Night storms are sometimes the scariest of all because, quite simply, you can't see a thing, just the lightning in the sky. The part where you know you're in trouble is when the stillness hits all around. There is sometimes a rather eerie silence, like you know the monster is there but are wondering where it will strike. Then, right upon the footsteps of the stillness, the wind will come and the trees will rustle and bend, and then one of the most awful sounds of all can usually be heard: the roaring of a freight train.

These sounds are imprinted on a child very early on when growing up in West Texas. You come to know them all too well. There are those people who are terrified of this, who have been way too close to the brink of this destruction, and there are others who have never been there and who simply do not know what these tumbling white clouds can do.

☆ ☆ ☆

One such person was my Aunt Madge; she had spent way too much time living up North and was really never that close to an actual tornado. One particular spring she came to visit us, and, of course, we had a good storm.

Aunt Madge was quite calm, but my mother was not. I was in the closet where I sat amidst my grandmother's dusters and sweaters. Mercifully, Grandmother was away at the time, so she didn't have to scrunch in there with me. She didn't like tight spaces at all.

My mother was in the kitchen wringing her hands, and Aunt Madge was just hungry.

"Where did I put the chicken salad?" she asked as she dug in the refrigerator.

"Salad?" asked Mother incredulously.

"Do we have any grapes?" asked Aunt Madge.

THUNK! THUNK! THUNK! The hail pelted against the window.

"We've got to see about building a cellar," said Mother.

"A cellar?" asked Madge. "Do you want to do some canning?"

"No, I want a hole to get in," said Mother. Outside the wind howled and inside the closet, I got stuck on my grandma's bumblebee pin. Limbs broke and sirens wailed. I noticed a stack of *True Story* magazines hidden in the corner of the closet.

"What was that?" asked Aunt Madge.

"Oh, not to worry. A cow just blew by the window," said my mother using sarcasm to ease her nerves.

"Oh, good Lord, how the wind does blow here!" said

Aunt Madge as she munched on her sandwich. "Have we any chocolate chip cookies?"

I fully expected my mother to join me in the closet and leave Aunt Madge to forage amidst the ruins of the house, but as good luck would have it, no tornado that day. There would be many more times in the future when our little town would lay smack dab in the path of violence. So far, the funnels have managed to find their way around it, so folks just keep hoping that will always be the case. It has seemingly been an odd afterthought of nature to finish big. Many times when the storm blows over, the sun comes out, and the wind dies down, and it looks like nothing happened at all.

38 Dena Kay

Dena Kay had a radio that was much more than just a transistor radio. This one had a pull-out antenna, and through it we could reach all kinds of places, including ones that sounded foreign. We used to hang out on the porch and tune into KOMA in Oklahoma City. They had pretty good music there, and they played many of our favorite songs. Lots of times we would start an evening by making chocolate crackers for radio time. Dena Kay knew just how to make the hot chocolate sauce that we poured over saltines, Zesty Crackers, of course, if we had them. Then we would go out, sit on the back of the car, and listen to music.

"Who was the guy who wrote you that letter?" I asked her one night.

"Gosh, I don't even know him," she said. "He is some darn convict in a prison!"

"Oh no! I sure hope Daddy doesn't find out that you're writing a convict."

"I don't know him. I'm not writing him, either," she retorted. "Somebody gave him my address as a practical joke."

"Somebody else in jail?"

"No, somebody who was visiting. Somebody in the jail. Probably that Russell Rogers. It sounds like him."

After such discussions, we would go inside and sometimes watch the late, late movie that came on TV. There were a lot of war movies that came on, highlighting every historic epoch, featuring a cast of Greeks, Romans, the Anglo-Saxons, and, of course, the cowboys and Indians. Dena Kay never minded being cooped up with the television, but I was way too active to sit and watch it all the time.

One winter we were snowed in, and the only thing on television was a horror movie that involved a girls school. As luck would have it, all the girls in the school were being murdered, which was right up Dena Kay's alley as she was a big fan of the macabre and this murder movie was almost as good as werewolves and *Dark Shadows*. We had what seemed to be movie month, with the cold, gray weather just hanging on. I thought I was gonna have to mail myself to California or Florida, or wherever there was sunshine and no girls schools.

Dena Kay was the most cantankerous of us all, whereas Beth Ann was nice, and I was more practical.

Dena Kay was just an ordinary girl living an ordinary life in the country and finally growing into an ordinary young woman. There was nothing remarkable about her: Dena Kay has her own small place in history and time and in the story of life. She was my sister, who duly tortured me when I was young, but who later served as my support throughout my own turbulent teenage years.

Dena Kay and I shared a lot of things together that I would end up missing when she was gone. For some reason, rural areas have high rates of car accidents. I've never really understood this because there aren't that many people around, but sometimes all you need is one car and one person and one moment. Many of these rural roads are narrow and winding and hard to navigate at night and in the rain. It was during one such storm that Dena Kay was making her way back home after visiting a friend. I don't really know what happened. It was dark and slick, and the car spun out of control and flipped, and my sister became a statistic for the State of Texas under the newspaper heading of fatal traffic accidents in rural areas. And that is how her story ended.

39 Ernesto Comes Home

After years of hanging in the beautiful state, with all the beautiful people, Ernesto decided it was time to go home, but his car had a problem. He pulled into the Dub's Garage where two mechanics were working on stacks of cars that were all along the side of the garage area. There were cars of all sizes and models there: hoods open, up on racks, all over the place.

Leroy and Vince, the head mechanics, came out to meet him.

"Brake fluid . . . Everywhere . . . Yep, that's it, all right," said Leroy.

"That's it," echoed Vince.

"What?" said Ernesto.

"Yep, it looks like the master cylinder," said Leroy picking his teeth and tossing his ponytail over his shoulder.

"Yes, indeed," said Vince wiping oil on his jeans, "I'm afraid that's what it is, the master cylinder."

"What the heck is that?" asked Ernesto.

"Well, it's bad, all right . . . your brakes. It's your brakes."

"Wow, how much is that?"

"Dunno yet. I'll be able to tell you shortly."

"Man, I just wanna go home."

"You leavin'?"

"Yep, I wanna go back for now," said Ernesto.

"What about the big time?" asked Vince.

"It's just hard right now. I have to work so much, and it doesn't pay nothing," said Ernesto.

"That's the truth!" said Leroy.

"And those pink rocks?" asked Vince pointing in the backseat.

"Quartz," said Ernesto.

"What's that wire wrapped around them?" asked Vince.

"Those are quartz sculptures, my specialty," said Ernesto. "They emit positive ions."

"Do what???" asked Leroy.

"To change my Karma," said Ernesto. Leroy looked at Vince.

"Let's get to those brakes. He's been out here too long," said Vince.

40 The Superhighway Ends an Era

For a brief time, the old Roy Ray Theater, which was a walk-in, opened up its doors to see what it could do in Viney, Texas. It had once been a skating rink, but the magic of that had eventually faded. We had to try it out, of course, but it simply didn't have the allure of the drive-in. Besides, nobody could have the added excuse of travel time to stay out later. There was something missing in Old Roy Ray, but you could throw popcorn at obnoxious classmates when the camera person turned out the lights to run the movie.

In the South, we know good food, and Viney had its share of joints. Beth Ann and Dena Kay used to take me to the Sugar Shack for a chocolate malt, one of our favorite after-movie past times. They had the best hamburgers and French fries to go with it, hot and salty and maybe a tad bit on the greasy side. I thought the Sugar Shack was famous because there was even a song out about it, but Dena Kay informed me, as she was always apt to do, that the song was not about this place, rather some other place that existed maybe alongside a Discount Food Store where some guy would go and drink coffee and hit on the waitresses. I guess the world was lucky to have more than one Sugar Shack.

We had some people from up North who came to visit relatives one summer, and they were just obsessed with the way we ate here. They went on and on about fried food, and my mother told them that sure thing, we fried anything that moved and many things that didn't. They kept asking me if we ate grits, and I had no idea what in the heck grits were, although I would never totally rule out any kind of food, being quite fond of it as I was.

So I asked Cotton Peabody down at Bailey's Grocery because he was the meat cutter there and he had a girlfriend who really liked to eat. In fact, he had nicknamed his lady love, the "Big Healthy Girl," which I thought was quite okay being that she was so stout and all. He was the only person around that could tell me what grits were and how to make them, and he told me that "sure 'nough, they aren't bad." Later I asked my nanny if she had ever tried grits. She said no. She had tried pickled okra and that was quite enough.

41 The House

I never knew at the time, when I was just a small, blonde girl, just how much a house could mean. My grandparents' farm has long grown over; the house burned down. The sand is still there; droughts and floods come and go. The land looks the same if you stare at it long enough. Mostly there's just an emptiness in those sandy hills. These days the rattlesnakes and coyotes have completely taken over.

I pull up in front of what used to be my grandmother's house at 430 West B Street. Now forlorn, vacant, and questioning. A lady bought it from my mother a few years ago, but she has already moved on. I hated selling that house; I'll bet I walked through it a million times, going in and out of the tiny rooms, remembering my family, those who had gone on and beyond these borders. Just a small, wood-frame house that stood as a beacon of comfort, a symbol of home base, a place that I thought I could always go back to and never imagined being without.

Here inside the walls of that little house, my cousins and I could still pretend; my sisters could have their friends over; I could hide in the old garage or climb on top of it. In this house, Sunday dinners were cooked with the loving, nurturing hands of my grandmother who painstakingly spent hours in the kitchen baking up homemade hot rolls, black-eyed peas, and roast beef. Miss Lola loved to cook for everybody. Her cooking was legendary. It still is to me and will live on in eternity.

At 430 West B Street, I could sit on the front porch like I did a million times and stare down the road. I would find it a little more desolate in this decade, but the landmarks are still there: the post office, the store that used to be the M-System, the paths my grandmother and I walked down, the now eroded sidewalks that stare back. I can almost hear my grandmother remark, as she said to me once, "I have no idea why I have lived this long."

This little place in the world is significant in my mind and will still always be that to me. If you go the other way on West B Street, you'll find the elementary and high schools, remodeled and revamped, but still familiar to those who once knew them.

Inside this house, my dreams and memories still live: naptime in the middle of the day, daylight seeping through the shuttered blinds, the hum of the evaporative air conditioner, the pink bathroom that Lacy Jean meticulously painted. The days I spent getting ready to go to the public swimming pool, both as an excited little kid and later as a teenager jamming out with Elton John on the stereo, are all stored neatly in the back bedroom.

The weather the house has seen: cold, hard, winter days, looking out into the snow, the flood where the streets turned to rivers, and, of course, tornado season. Many visitors were entertained at the house on West B Street. My grandmother, the eternal hostess, made sure that no one left hungry. I see them now as yesterday, waving goodbye, long gone, but still near enough that I can almost touch them right here.

I have worked on this house with my bare hands. I have painted it inside and out, I have pulled marauding trumpet vines, repaired the fence, and tried to repair the porches. I hung on with a relentless physical fervor, trying to win the war of the Present destroying a most perfect thing from the Past, but time and decay continue, and we are all at the mercy of progress through the new and unknown. Lives have changed, patterns have been lost, yet many people persevere and fight the good fight, every day. The Sandman lives on—blowing in the wind.

I look over the little town that was once mine, and I make a decision. The trouble with downsizing is you have an ever stretching and constricting economy, sorta like an earthworm inching along. In this economic channel, the focus and everything that matters seem to be based on the number of widgets that can be sold as depicted by the whole supply and demand curve. This was what I later learned when I went to college.

And so it has been that the supply and demand curve hit these little rural towns hard and leveled them out pretty well. Hospitality and grace are in plentiful supply, but the demand seems to have dried up. Many people had to go and sell their farms, and their widgets, too. Move out. The end of simplicity.

Of all the businesses that have come and gone, I think I miss the auto supply store the most. The auto building just does not look quite right vacant. It just begs for something to inhabit it. I notice this as it sits in the middle of the town, jutted out in the shape of a triangle on its own peninsula. I know that Raymond probably misses the store, too, since it was the only place to get parts for miles around. You could just walk in and tell the man behind the counter whatever part you needed, and he would come back with a fan belt, brake pad, or anything else.

I used to sit next to my grandmother on her sofa, and she would tell me about her life. Sometimes we would both fall asleep listening to the hum of the swamp cooler in her living room. I liked sitting in front of the cooler and taking in the smell of water and straw along with the cold blast of air that came out of it. My grandmother would take up a book and read to me, and I was able to go many places and not simply be restricted to my own little corner of the world. Grandmother liked to put her own spin on stories and sometimes would underscore that with a bit of Bible scripture, even then she was exhibiting a quality that I later learned the intellectually elite would refer to as "artistic license."

In the course of these events, I have learned the full meaning of becoming the essence of one's own experiences. The Sixties were a turbulent time in history, but not my history. It was a decade marked by explicit destruction and protest, yet war and death were very far from my little town. Those things did not reach into my world; I knew of their existence from scattered ghostly flashes of television, and I would come to be glad to have the freedom and security of a small-town existence.

 **42 And Finally . . .**

And so it is, somewhere out there in the vast spinning continuum of time, exists a snapshot series of my sisters and me fused together in this moment of history. The Sixties were the hallmark of a carefree childhood for me now, long passed while the dry, windy landscape of small-town Texas continues on in the evolution of time.

When they finally tore down that drive-in movie, they did much more than change an era. They took a little piece of Hollywood glamour out of that cow pasture. Now it's just as dark as can be at night. No more Phyllis Diller to dance around in pink feathers. No more teenagers piling out of cars and sneaking into the movies. The swings, the snack bar, and speakers are all gone, and it's just a pasture of coastal Bermuda grass.

Such is the overall shape of rural Texas at the present: superhighways come through, jobs go out, and farming goes to the dogs. Ernesto and I, we share a bond: this time and place. The time he spent chasing Santana all over California was the time I spent drinking cold colas in those teeny, tiny bottles and eating Baby Ruth candy bars. I will always feel the constant presence here of my family, those I loved dearly who have left this life for the great, greener farmlands beyond.

And with this satisfaction culminates in the careful curation of memories now airborne and flying free in the stout West Texas wind. So I smile ruefully and wave goodbye to the past, to Dena Kay's echoes all through the now desolate little town, and to Ernesto. I don't think he sees me anymore as he is almost looking through me.

Sometimes the solitude here jumps up and screams in your face when the people shut themselves up inside their houses and barricade their little town against the ravages of a cruel world. Sometimes when the wind is calm and the clouds turn purple pink in a picturesque western sunset, one can find certain serenity and accept the brief peace that this small part of Texas offers. It is during such times that I walk down the sidewalk and I wonder to myself if Beth Ann ever stops to remember anymore about the days when her hair was too big and her skirts were too short.

Acknowledgements

Dancing with the Sandman is a vibrant imaginative, fictional journey through a past era that explores life in a small town in Texas. I have sincere gratitude to many who helped make this journey through time possible. I would like to thank Craig Paylor for all of his love, support, and suggestions for this book. I would like to express my love and gratitude to my children who inspire me every day: Amber, Andrea, Austen, Jordan, and Justin. All my love and thanks to three very special grandchildren: Hayley, Tristan, and Preston. I would like to thank my publisher, Patricia Landy at Crystal Publishing for her support and encouragement, creative advice, and close reading of the text. I would like to thank the editors, Keri de Deo, Bonnie Walker, and Claire Shepherd for editing the manuscript, correcting errors and making outstanding suggestions that have greatly enhanced the quality of this work. I would like to express my appreciation to all my fellow WordPress writer and blogger friends who continue to inspire me in all things concerning the written word. Lastly, I would like to posthumously thank my mother for her strength, intelligence, sense of humor and independence that has continued to encourage and motivate me along the road of life.

About the Author

L. T. Garvin is the pen name of Lana Broussard. She writes fiction, poetry, and essays and publishes a blog. Her poetry has recently appeared in *Wax Poetry & Art*, waxpoetryart.com and *Every Writers Every Day Poems*, everywritersresource.com. An avid reader and long-time literature fan, L.T. has been writing from a very early age. She holds a Master's Degree in Library Science from Texas Woman's University, Teaching Certification for English/Language Arts, and a Bachelor's Degree in Business from Midwestern State University. L.T.'s work has appeared in *Texas Writer's Journal*. L.T. resides in Wichita Falls, Texas where the weather is hot and sports competition is tough. In her spare time, she enjoys photography, jewelry crafting, genealogy, her assorted felines, gardening, antiques, and revamping a 1930s house.